WEST OF THE LAW

Law in the Red Rock Country was argued with Colt .45's. No man knew that better than lawyer Tom Chisholm. He had refused to play ball with Symes Gallister and found himself victim of the sweetest frame-up west of the Rockies. Tom was fighting for his life, and in a way, for his country. If one crook could run a town to suit himself, then America's young democracy was lost!

WEST OF THE LAW

Al Cody

CHIVERS LARGE PRINT
Bath, England

CURLEY LARGE PRINT
Hampton, New Hampshire

Library of Congress Cataloging-in-Publication Data available

British Library Cataloguing in Publication Data available

This Large Print edition is published by Chivers Press, England, and by Curley Large Print, an imprint of Chivers North America, 1994.

Published by arrangement with Donald MacCampbell, Inc.

U.K. Hardcover ISBN 0 7451 2326 0
U.K. Softcover   ISBN 0 7451 2337 6
U.S. Hardcover ISBN 0 7927 2117 9
U.S. Softcover   ISBN 0 7927 2116 8

Copyright, 1947, by Dodd, Mead and Company, Inc.

Printed in Great Britain

WEST OF THE LAW

CHAPTER ONE

The stage, its once flashing red trappings now rusty and dust-covered, had been late in pulling out from the Four Corners. Consequently the fifteen miles between the Corners and the huddle of shacks which marked Boxelder Creek had been hard ones, hard alike on the teams and on the passengers, crowded sardinelike in the swaying, jolting confines. Tom Chisholm had cursed under his breath, and his resolution to travel like the veriest tenderfoot had been severely tried. It would be so much easier to go by saddle.

So it had been a double relief, where half a dozen boxelder trees broke the flat monotony of prairie, to alight and stretch his legs, and to observe thankfully that the stage from the west was not yet in.

Apparently it was coming, however, judging by an enlarging trail of dust which sprang up, genielike, along the road, then hung above it like a long quivering sigh. But as the dust neared, Chisholm saw that it was not the stage but a lone horseman who was bedeviling it, riding hard. His cayuse was lather-streaked, crusted with dusty mud. The rider was a tall man, who seemed sprouting out of his clothes like a weed, and there was impatience in the line of his jaw, a cruelty about the thin-set

1

mouth which the condition of his horse did not belie.

The driver of the Red Eagle stage, from which Chisholm had just alighted, hailed him as Rance. And there was both a deference and a marked lack of enthusiasm, oddly mingling, in his attitude.

For a few moments they conferred earnestly, low-toned, the cayuse standing with legs braced wide apart, head lowered, its heavy breath raising little spurts of dust. By then, the stage from the west, showing a faded blue beneath its own whitish, all-pervading dust, was coming into sight. It would turn here and go west again, as the other would swing back east, marking the division of two lines.

Chisholm regarded it without particular interest. It looked to be as much of a torture chamber as the vehicle which he had just quitted, and his resolution stretched thin. There was a livery stable here, and he could rent or buy a horse—

Then his interest quickened a little. A handful of passengers were alighting from this newest arrival. They would transfer to the eastbound stage, just as he would to the west. One of them was a woman.

There was nothing extraordinary about that fact, for, in point of accuracy, two other women had alighted as well. But they were like quiet border plants, fringing an exotic orchid; and they were together, just as she was plainly

2

alone. Yet, alone or in a crowd, there was something about her which seemed to draw eyes like a magnet.

It might have been, in part, her beauty—though she seemed a cold, aloof brunette, a trifle tall for a woman, and she walked as though unconscious, or perhaps disdainful, of the covert glances sent her way. But it was more of something else, it seemed to Chisholm, which set her apart—as though she shunned the world and wished to withdraw from it, like a wounded animal seeking covert.

That was a ridiculous simile to use in connection with a beautiful woman of not more than twenty, he reflected, yet it persisted in his mind. He saw her cross to the other waiting stage of the Red Eagle. She had started to open the door when she was stopped by the driver. He was deferential, but firm, refusing to allow her to enter.

Swift anger blossomed in her cheeks, though her voice was not raised. Chisholm, from where he stood, could not catch what she said. Then he saw that she was thrusting money at the driver, was pleading with him to accept it, to take her with him on this trip outward. To all alike, protestations, bribery or pleadings, he was deaf.

A moment later, closing the door firmly, he jumped to his box, kicked off the brake and, with fresh horses dragging the stage, was away in a new-rising cloud of dust. The woman

3

stood staring after the departing vehicle as though she had been denied entry to paradise.

Chisholm was more than puzzled, though somehow, he felt, there must be a connection between the hurried arrival of the man Rance and the refusal of the eastbound stage to take her farther.

Yet it seemed inconceivable that a passenger should come this far and be denied accommodations on the next stage of the journey, more especially since the Red Eagle was less crowded now than it had been on the incoming trip. Had she been a child, a possible runaway, the thing might have been understandable. But she was a woman, and of the age of responsibility. Yet somehow she reminded him now of a little child, lost and forlorn.

The thing which had first struck him as queer was increasingly so now. From the almost forced casualness with which the bystanders disregarded her, it was apparent that most of them knew her and understood what this was all about. She appeared to be very close to tears, but now her head lifted a little, her chin was outthrust stubbornly. It was plain to Chisholm that she had no intention of taking this, whatever it was, without a fight. He felt like cheering.

Her bag, a rather heavy one, had been set off the blue stage by now, and she picked it out of the pile, started with a determined tread down

4

the single short street which made up this town, if such it could be called. There was the stage house and livery barn, a saloon, and a couple of other buildings. One served, apparently, as store, post office and dwelling house. There was nothing beyond them.

Apparently it was not her intention to go to any of them, but to walk, since that seemed to be the only way—to trudge in the direction of the departing stage. Chisholm watched her, uneasily, wondering what would happen next.

It was not long in coming. Rance, who had beaten the eastbound stage here by minutes, came out of the saloon now, wiping his mustache. More than ever, on foot, he seemed to sprout out of his clothes in a jerky fashion. He saw her, stared for a moment, then overtook her in a few quick steps. With an air half-deferential, half-assertive, he put his fingers on her arm—and was promptly slapped viciously.

'Keep your hands off me, Jud Rance!' she snapped. And her voice, though still repressed, was boiling with pent-up fury.

Rance nodded, awkwardly.

'Jus' as you say, Mis' Gallister,' he conceded. 'Only you're to get back on the stage, you know, an' go home!'

He had placed himself in front of her, so that, perforce, she halted. But her eyes, deeply blue, as Chisholm saw now, blazed at him in a scorching fury.

'I'll die first!' she stormed.

'I'm right sorry, about this, Mis' Gallister,' Rance went on, uneasily. 'But I got orders. You got to go back.'

For a moment, she stood there, then her eyes, half-appealing, half-defiant, swept the group near the waiting stage. Everyone had been watching, but still with that air of appearing not to do so. Not one of them would meet her gaze, except Chisholm, whose curiosity was at a lively point by now. For an instant his eyes met hers, and there was something in her own which went through him as the shivering of lightning had once done, striking a wire fence which he had been standing near. Her voice, addressed to everyone and no one in particular, was bitter.

'Is there no one in this country who will help a woman? No one who believes in fair play—or who has the courage of his convictions?'

'I'm sorry, Mis' Gallister, but you got to take the stage back,' Rance persisted.

Chisholm stepped forward, sweeping off his hat. Instinct and training, old and new alike, warned him that he might do better to keep out of this, but in the face of such an appeal he could not stand back. He saw Rance's eyes on him, quick and speculative, faintly hostile.

'What seems to be the trouble, Madam?' he asked. 'Is there anything that I can do?'

For an instant, she surveyed him in silence, faint surprise in her eyes, and with, he guessed,

6

a little of disappointment as well. She was slender and, as he had seen before, a trifle tall for a woman, whereas Chisholm knew himself as not only under the average in height for a man but of a look which seldom produced a favorable first impression.

Standing so, he topped her by a scant inch, and his hair was already thinning a little in front, despite the fact that he was her senior by not more than four or five years. He was, so far as looks went, a tenderfoot, but otherwise, and anywhere, just one of the crowd—not one to catch the eye. But he had found that to be an asset, that people should underestimate him at the first.

Then her eyes warmed a little, in recognition of the gesture. Her voice was still cool, steady.

'The trouble is that I wish to travel out of this country, and these people'—her eyes, her voice were derisive, but hate-charged as well—'they are determined that I shall not go.'

Rance made a gesture behind her back, for Chisholm's benefit. A slight shrug, a significant tapping of his own head. Chisholm was incredulous. If this girl was mentally incompetent, she certainly gave no sign of it. She was speaking again, directly to him.

'I am not a free agent,' she said, 'though of legal age and knowing my own mind. But everyone in this country is afraid of the man who—who calls himself my husband. If there was one real man in this whole stretch of country—one who could not be bought or sold, as we do with cattle—'

Chisholm was perplexed, distressed, and infuriated. There was something wrong here, that was easy to see, and his impulse was to help her. But the thing, as he had seen instantly, was not a matter for easy solution.

'Mrs—Gallister,' he said tentatively, 'I would like to help you. Perhaps I can, if I am permitted to look into this. I am a lawyer, and it almost seems, from what little I have seen and heard, that legal action may be required to straighten this out.'

Now she was looking at him with quickened interest. So was Rance, and there was a quick hostility in his look now as well. He spoke again, insistently.

'Stage is ready to start back, Mis' Gallister. You'll have to be gettin' on.'

'Will you help me?' she appealed again, to Chisholm. 'I do have a case—and I'll pay you well—if you will. Please! I—I'll go back to Red Rock,' she added. 'And I do need a lawyer—a good one, and an honest one.'

'You've hired yourself a lawyer, at least, and I hope I'm an honest one,' Chisholm agreed. 'That is, if you still feel that way about it after we've had a chance to talk. As it happens, Red Rock is where I had planned to hang my shingle out. Perhaps it would be better to return, at least for the present.'

She looked deep into his eyes for a moment,

and what she saw there seemed to encourage her. For a moment her face was transfigured by a rare smile.

'Thank you,' she agreed. 'I will. And you have the look of an honest man—though there are others who look so,' and her lips curled in sudden bitterness. 'But I do want you to help me—not to let me down. If you will, I promise that it will be worth your while.'

She turned toward the stage, and he helped her into it, turned to pick up his own bag. But as he was about to follow her inside, the ungainly Rance was overtowering him, Rance's hand was urgently on his shoulder.

'I'd ride on top, if I was you, Mister,' he suggested, and there was the hint of a snarl in his voice. 'Pretty crowded inside.'

It was not so much a suggestion as an order, Chisholm knew. Jud Rance overtowered him by at least five inches and outweighed him by half a hundred pounds. But Chisholm's fingers had been itching for the last five minutes, and the big man's supercilious jaw was a perfect target.

Chisholm's fist traveled a short, direct arc. Not for nothing had he been captain of the boxing team at college for the last two years. Rance rocked as though hit by a sledge hammer. He wavered a moment, then his knees buckled and he went down in the dust of the road, out cold.

The driver, a man with a cud of tobacco

pouched in his cheek so that he had the perpetual look of mumps, had started to close the door. But now he stared, his Adam's apple bobbing violently. Calmly, Chisholm stepped past him and inside. He took the vacant place beside Mrs Gallister, and was rewarded by a quick, ravishing smile which again transformed her whole face.

'It looks,' she murmured, 'as though a man *had* come to this country at last!'

CHAPTER TWO

During the next dozen miles, Chisholm learned only that she lived by herself, in town, not with her husband on his big Sunset Ranch. His own opinion had been that it would be better not to discuss anything before the other frankly curious passengers, and she shared it, as he could see. She had volunteered the suggestion that, once he was settled in town, they could discuss things then.

Otherwise they rode in silence—a hush broken only by the creaking of the stage, the rasp of iron-shod tires on stones, the click of hoofs and the occasional hoarse voice of the driver. The other passengers were quiet as well, as though the presence of Chisholm and this woman had set a constraint upon them.

There was something strange here, as Chisholm had already sensed, and, underneath

10

it all, something ominous as well. Which did not worry him. He was ready to do battle—legally, and for the right. His mind went back, briefly, with only a shadow of the old bitterness, to his boyhood on the range, half a thousand miles from this country, to the horror of range war, the impact of red violence. Some had said, bluntly, that he had been afraid, when he had left that country. And that thought, the old accusation, had rankled through the years.

Now he knew that it meant nothing, because it was untrue. It wasn't physical violence that he was afraid of; it was soul-sickness that men should use such senseless methods in trying to solve their difficulties. Out of bloodshed grew only bitterness and sorrow.

It had seemed to him, then, that the way to solve such problems was by legal and orderly processes, to arrive at justice with equity and mercy. So he had gone away and had trained himself for that, and now, in a land still marked by violence, his chance was at hand.

A chance to help one in need. But he knew that it was more than the chance alone, or her need, which gave him now such a sense of exhilaration, which was out of all proportion to the thing itself, so far. As her first glance had been like the tingle of the lightning, so was her whole personality vibrant, alive. Sitting beside her became an adventure.

Conscious that his mind was not behaving as

that of a well-trained legal expert, Chisholm stared outside and tried to readjust himself. He had picked Red Rock for his future scene of operations mostly because it had sounded well to the ear, which was a frivolous, almost a romantic way, rather than sound business judgment. For beyond its name he knew nothing of it. But here was a matter which quite plainly required some sort of legal settlement, and that was his business.

The country was still unprepossessing, though its level flatness was gradually giving way to rolling hills. But hereabouts there was still the look of alkali, the water was still brackish and unpleasant. Houses were few and far between.

They had covered half the distance to Red Rock when a pound of hoofs sounded, then Jud Rance came galloping up, no longer ungainly in the saddle. He passed the stage, with a black look toward it, and kept on, without regard to the condition of his nearly exhausted horse.

But no one spoke until they were pulling in to Red Rock, which was an agreeable surprise—a well laid out little town, a county seat, with neat, well-painted houses and a good business section. Then, half timidly, the girl laid her hand lightly on his arm.

'You won't forget—you won't let them talk you out of helping me—or buy you off—or bluff you out?' she asked. 'I need your help—

desperately!'

'You can count on me,' Chisholm replied, and meant it. She seemed to read it in his eyes, more than in the words, for she nodded quietly.

'I will—I am,' she said, and stepped down to the street. Alighting in turn, Chisholm saw that she was already across it, walking swiftly, with never a backward look. The driver of the stage stared after her, shifted his cud to the opposite cheek, and leaned toward him.

'Stranger,' he said, and his voice was guarded but friendly, 'my name's Mosby—Lick Mosby. I saw what you done to Jud, back there. Mighty good work, too. But that'll only get you in trouble, around here. This is Symes Gallister's country, and Rance is Gallister's man, same as plenty more. The stage pulls on west in five minutes. If you like good health, you better just ride along with it.'

'This is as far as I go,' Chisholm said, a little sharply; then, conscious of the other's friendliness, turned back. 'Thanks just the same, Lick.'

He turned then to survey the street. A couple of blocks down he could see the courthouse, bowered among big cottonwoods, built of native red rock, looking imposing and cool. There was a pump and trough closer at hand, and he took a drink, conscious that the water was better here, yet still with a curiously brackish taste.

Closer at hand, too, were what appeared to

13

be a combination of saloon and hotel, two of them; and, since there was apparently little choice between, he turned to the nearest, The Last Chance.

The saloon was on the first floor, the rooms on the second. He secured a room, washed up, then went in search of a restaurant and supper. He sought a small, secluded table in a well-filled room, and noted that the story of the Four Corners had already preceded him. Men took oblique looks at him, then went on talking a little faster than before. He was not particularly surprised when, with his meal half over, another man slid, with a murmur of apology, into the chair opposite him.

He was a tall man, as most of them ran in this country. Lean and hard and competent, smooth shaven, and he did not even glance at the menu. Instead he smiled at the waitress and told her to bring him whatever was good, and then he smiled again at Chisholm.

'That's the best way to do, here,' he said. 'Though it's still a tossup.'

Chisholm had been around enough to know that this was no accident, this man coming to his table. So he responded, and after a moment the other man held out his hand.

'Dunning's my name,' he said. 'Tate Dunning. You're new hereabouts, aren't you?'

'I just arrived a little while ago,' Chisholm agreed, and gave his own name. 'Lawyer,' he added dryly.

'Lawyer, did you say?' Dunning made it sound as if he was both surprised and pleased. 'Say, I'm twice as glad to see you, Mr Chisholm. Maybe this is my lucky day. And maybe the same for a friend of mine.'

'Yes?' Chisholm was politely interested.

'I have a friend who needs a good lawyer, now, and who has asked me to get him one. Maybe you're it.'

Chisholm's eyebrows rose.

'Aren't there other lawyers in town?' he asked.

'Several,' Dunning agreed. 'One of them, the best, is on the other side. Two of them, my friend declined to have. He's a bit stubborn at times. I tried the remaining one, just a little while ago, but he has to be out of town for the next few days. I was wondering what to do when I came in here.'

'Are a few days so important?' Chisholm wondered.

'Plenty, when the case comes up in the morning,' Dunning said promptly, 'and when a man's neck is threatened by the noose—' he shrugged.

'As bad as that?'

'Just that bad. Would you be interested?'

'What makes you think I'd be a good gamble?' Chisholm asked.

Dunning leaned forward gravely.

'Any lawyer, in my opinion, would be better than for Brick to try to defend himself,' he explained. 'But as I say, he's a bit stubborn where he dislikes a man. And of the two others available, he says they're tin horns. Also, to be more specific, I'm not a bad judge of men. I have a hunch that you might do a good job. Added to that, I'm a gambler. Since we have to gamble, in any case, it's better to gamble on the cards you haven't seen than on what's in your hand—if the hand you hold isn't good enough to win with. You may draw aces.'

'What's this case like?' Chisholm asked.

'A murder case. Brick Hogarth is charged with first degree murder. He claims that it's all a mistake, that someone else in the crowd did the shooting, but because he's hot-headed and the two had been quarreling, Brick is accused. The cards are stacked against him, and he's likely to be railroaded, but Brick is my friend, and I believe his story. I want him to have a fair chance, a good lawyer, and all the rights that he's entitled to.'

'When did this shooting take place?'

'This afternoon.'

'This afternoon?' Chisholm echoed, aghast. 'And the trial is to be tomorrow? That's ridiculous.'

'That's the way it is,' Dunning said grimly. 'Brick wanted it that way himself. He's young—just a kid, really, and hot-headed. Told the judge at the preliminary hearing that he couldn't stand to be shut up for long, waiting. And Brick was lucky that the sheriff

16

got to him when he did. Otherwise he'd have had no trial at all.'

Chisholm shivered a little. So his prospective client had escaped a lynching by so narrow a margin as that? All that his training had ingrained in him rose up in revolt. The law was the law, and a man deserved a fair trial on the merits of the case.

He was half inclined to take this, for that if for no other reason. But he had expected a trick when Dunning had come to his table, and it would still pay to be cautious.

'We might call on your friend when we finish supper, and see what he thinks of me,' he suggested. 'By the way, do you know a Mrs Gallister?'

Dunning looked at him a little queerly.

'Mrs Symes Gallister?' he repeated. 'The former Molly Benton? But I've heard of the way you bopped Jud Rance and laid him out cold—everybody has. Yes, I know her.'

'What's the setup?' Chisholm demanded.

'One where you can burn your fingers easy, Chisholm. I'm not going to try and advise you about that—it's none of my business. She married Symes Gallister here a few weeks ago but has refused to live with him. She claims trickery and fraud and tried to get an annulment, but failed. I don't pretend to know all the ins and outs of it. But they say that— well, that she suffers from hallucinations. Gallister seems to be trying to let her have her way and do pretty much as she pleases, but to try and look after her at the same time, just to see that she gets along all right. As I say, it's complicated, and—well, Gallister owns Sunset, which is saying a lot in this country.'

He ended abruptly, and Chisholm could see that he did not care to say more. He had inferred, plainly enough, that Gallister was probably sensitive on that score and adverse to outside interference. His frankness had impressed Chisholm favorably. Dunning stood up.

'Shall we go and brighten Brick's evening a bit?' he asked.

Brick Hogarth told a convincing story. He was surprisingly young, younger even than Chisholm, fair-haired, very pleasant. He admitted that he had quarreled with the dead man, that the other man had started to draw a gun on him.

'And I'm quick with a gun, and pretty good,' he said, with disarming modesty. 'I suppose I'd have killed him in another half-second to save myself. But I knew that I was better than he was, and I was waitin' as long as I could— though I guess I was startin' to draw. Folks saw that.'

He shook his head.

'Right then, a shot rang out, and he dropped, dead. Somebody in the crowd, I reckon. But it did look like me—folks said it was. And here I am, with plenty willin' to swear that they saw me do it.'

'But your gun?' Chisholm demanded. 'If it hadn't been fired—'

Hogarth grinned crookedly.

'That's the blazes of it,' he admitted. 'I'd took a shot at a magpie, comin' in to town, a little spell before, and had been plumb careless, not to flip that empty out and reload. I'm not usually that careless—so nobody believes me. It's only my word. And when somebody says one thing, and you think you saw different, what are you going to believe? What you think you saw, or what somebody says—when that seems to make you out a liar? Here it's ten to one against me. That's what I'm up against.'

Chisholm was already planning. He liked Brick Hogarth and believed his story. This thing would take some doing, on such short notice, and would require some unorthodox handling. But a trick, if legitimately used, was fair enough. And this would take only a little time, the next morning. If it got him in the eye of the public, perhaps successfully, it might be a powerful lever with which to help Molly Gallister. And she would need help—while he would need all the leverage he could get, as he sensed.

The necessary ruse now was already taking shape in his mind. Outside the jail again, and since he would need help, he told his idea to Dunning. The tall cowboy listened, then roared with laughter.

19

'If you don't get tossed in the jail along with him, for contempt of court, and the rest of us along with you, maybe you'll have a case, at that,' he chuckled. 'But however it comes out, I guess I played the right hunch when I came to you, Chisholm. You'll go a long way in this country.'

CHAPTER THREE

Chisholm sat quietly, listening to the evidence as presented by the prosecution, raising no objections. McKinstry, the prosecutor, was a man inclined to slash and slash his way through, and he was making out a strong case. More than once he glanced at Chisholm in perplexity.

For all that, Chisholm remained calm. His cross-questioning of witnesses was brief and perfunctory. Not on that, with his meager knowledge of the case, could he hope to win, nor was he staking anything on that angle of it.

It was an ugly sounding thing, he conceded to himself, listening to the evidence. On the basis of such testimony as was being given he would probably vote for conviction, if he was in the jury box. But Brick Hogarth had assured him that he was innocent, and he liked the frank, open face of the boy, the ingenuous way he had of looking a man straight in the eye when he spoke. The idea that such a youngster, scarcely out of his teens, could be a killer was ridiculous.

Nor was the prosecution, Chisholm noted significantly, attempting to present any evidence of a prior bad record. Which probably meant that this, in any case, was a first offense. Chisholm's eyes strayed to the judge, seated behind the big bench, with the American flag spread across the wall behind him. If anything more had been needed to complete the picture of justice, working in orderly process, Judge Wood added that necessary touch.

He was a man in his early fifties, with dark hair which showed a slight tendency to curl, and it was graying around the fringes. His was a soldierly erectness, a benign, scholarly face. He was calm, his questions, when he leaned forward to probe more deeply into some point, penetrating and fair-minded. His voice was deep, richly resonant.

Chisholm smiled a little to himself. He knew that McKinstry was regarding him now with something approaching contempt, and that was the way he liked to have it. It never paid to underestimate your opponent.

He had only one regret, that he must resort to the ruse he had determined upon. With such a man as Wood on the bench, it seemed like an imposition upon good nature. But when a man's life was at stake, that was the thing of paramount importance.

21

He stood up, slowly, following the curt announcement that the prosecution rested. They had made a strong case, and he caught his client's eyes upon him, a little anxiously, and smiled reassuringly. Then he began to speak, and his own voice, beginning rather low, took on a timbre and resonance which caused heads to lift in surprise.

'Your Honor, and Gentlemen of the Jury,' he said, 'we have here, it seems to me, one more in the endless procession of those things which are not what they seem. My client is on trial for his life, and life is a very precious thing. There is the old injunction of an eye for and eye, and a tooth for a tooth. My learned colleague,' he bowed to the prosecutor, 'has been demanding just that, in the interests of justice.

'Like him, I am concerned that justice shall be done. But not that an innocent man should suffer. It has been made to appear that Brick Hogarth has killed a man. Yet the evidence is purely circumstantial, and again, I repeat, things are not what they seem. For instance—'

He raised his hand in an eloquent gesture, and as though that had been a signal, something happened. A man stood up in the middle of the crowded room and shouted something unintelligible. Judge Wood frowned and pounded on his desk, and the bailiff, jerked out of a daydream, crossed hastily to the still protesting onlooker. Then it happened.

Throwing off the bailiff's outreaching hand, the creator of the disturbance jerked a revolver. He raised it toward the big hanging lamp near the rear of the room. As the gun roared, the lamp shattered into a hundred pieces, and those of the crowd caught near it scurried frantically for safety.

Judge Wood came to his feet, pounding angrily for order. The bailiff seized the disturber, who was suddenly standing there, looking meek and a little scared, and led him forward. Order was restored, and the judge leaned forward sternly.

'I must ask you for the meaning of this unseemly demonstration,' he said, 'but that can come at another time. For the present, you will consider yourself under arrest for contempt of court. Bailiff, remove the prisoner, so that we can proceed with the trial.'

Chisholm turned to the judge and bowed.

'May the Court withhold judgment for a moment, in this instance, if you please,' he requested. 'I can explain this whole occurrence—which, I may add, ties in directly with the trial.'

Judge Wood regarded him frowningly for a moment. Then he relaxed a little.

'Your explanation had better be a good one, sir,' he warned. 'We are not accustomed to such methods in this court. You may explain.'

'Thank you, Your Honor. Mr Bailiff, will you kindly bring me the weapon which this gentleman has just used to shoot that lamp to pieces?'

The bailiff did so, having already taken possession of the gun. Chisholm took it, poised it for a moment on the palm of his hand, then handed it across to the judge.

'Your Honor,' he said, aware that everyone now was watching him tensely, including the prosecutor, 'I am sure that you are familiar with guns, so I will ask you to examine this one. It was apparent to everyone in this room, and I am certain that virtually everyone here would be prepared to swear, having seen it with their own eyes, that this gentleman drew this gun and shot that lamp to pieces. Is that not so?'

'It was plain enough,' Wood growled, a little angry.

'Exactly. May I inquire of the gentlemen of the jury if that is also their opinion?'

There could be no doubt on that point. Chisholm smiled, and now he seemed to take on added stature.

'Please examine the gun, Your Honor. I must confess to a ruse—in the interests of justice. You will see, I think, that no shot has been fired from the gun—though, with the bailiff beside the gentleman at the moment, and every moment since, it is plain that he could not have ejected an empty shell, nor reloaded it.'

A little puzzled, the judge broke open the gun, held it to the light, squinted through the barrel, twirling the cylinder in his fingers.

'As you say, this gun has not been fired—not recently, that is,' he agreed. 'There is no odor of powder smoke about it, the barrel is spotlessly clean, there are no empty shells. But what is the meaning of this?'

'As I say, it was a demonstration, in the interests of justice. We are prepared to pay for a new lamp, and all other damages. This act was staged at my request. This whole case—involving Brick Hogarth—hinges on one simple fact. That the witnesses for the prosecution believe, each of them, that they saw my client shoot down the victim in cold blood. They have testified to that effect. He insists that they did not see correctly. Mr Dunning, please come forward.'

Tate Dunning came, from where he had been standing near a doorway. In his hand he held a revolver.

'It was Mr Dunning, Your Honor, who shot the lamp at the proper moment,' Chisholm explained. 'But because everybody was watching this other man, and because they saw the gun in his hand, saw it pointed toward the lamp, and heard a shot, with the lamp breaking at that precise moment—I am sure that virtually every man and woman in this room, including even the jury and yourself, would have sworn, in all good faith, that he had fired the shot which smashed the lamp. Yet it was Mr Dunning who actually fired the shot, and no one the wiser.'

He bowed, smiling a little ironically.

'My point is that it is sometimes easy to be mistaken in what we see—or think we see. A man's life, I may remind you, is at stake, on precisely this issue. The defense rests.'

Everyone had grown deeply thoughtful. And the verdict, when it was brought in a little later, was 'Not guilty.'

Chisholm was pleasantly excited. He had received a mild reprimand from Judge Wood, in regard to carrying unorthodox methods to an extreme, but he could see that the judge had been favorably impressed. So had most of the crowd. Now he was known in Red Rock, and better than a score of ordinary cases could have made him.

CHAPTER FOUR

Chisholm was whistling softly between his teeth as he left the courtroom. He was not a conceited man, and the pride which he took was in an accomplishment rather than in himself. But things were working out better than he had dared hope for. With his reputation so enhanced at the start, on his first full day in Red Rock, he would have the prestige to act now for Molly Gallister. Presently he would go and see her and talk things over.

26

He was conscious that men were turning to watch him as he went along the street, but that was not to be wondered at. A man had faced the noose, with little prospect that the testimony against him could be shaken. But it had been done.

Chisholm reached his own room, up above the saloon, and stood for a moment in the bare, bleak hallway. Once he had established himself, and built up a good practice, he would find better lodgings. He turned the knob, went inside, and stopped at sight of Tate Dunning, lounging in the one chair which the room afforded. Dunning stood up, grinning at sight of him.

'You weren't around when I got here, so I thought I'd just make myself at home till you came,' he said easily. 'Congratulations, Chisholm. Your trick worked.'

Chisholm did not like the word. To him, that act there in the courtroom had been a demonstration of human fallacy, an example of how easily men could be mistaken. But he was not in a mood to argue about it.

'Hogarth goes free, at least,' he agreed.

'And that's what I came up here about,' Dunning added, and reached into his pocket. 'As I think I told you, Hogarth is my friend. He is grateful, and so am I—not to mention his employer. And the laborer, as the saying is, is worthy of his hire. Here is a little fee, on account.'

27

He extended a handful of crisp new twenty-dollar bills. Chisholm took them, a little surprised, and riffled them through. There were ten of them.

'This is considerably more than I would have thought of asking,' he confessed. 'And what did you mean by "On account"? He's out of this, now.'

'Brick's the sort who can stick his head back in trouble faster than a good lawyer can get him out,' Dunning said easily. 'Besides, it's really a retainer from our boss. He's very well pleased with the way you handled that case, Chisholm. That trick was a neat one. You're about the smartest man to hit this town in a long time, and the boss appreciates cleverness. These other lawyers—they have no imagination.'

'What are you talking about?' Chisholm demanded, irritated and puzzled. 'And who do you mean by the boss?'

'Who should I mean but Symes Gallister? When anybody talks of the boss, in this country, that's who they mean.'

Chisholm stared, wondering if the man was having a little joke. But it was plain enough that Dunning was in earnest. His own anger rose.

'See here, Dunning,' he protested, 'I took this case to defend an innocent man—or a man whom I believed to be innocent. I did that, to the best of my ability. But I was working for

Hogarth, not Gallister.'

'Of course, of course,' Dunning agreed soothingly. 'But when you work for Sunset, you work for the outfit. Not for any one man, unless you want to call Sunset Symes Gallister. For Sunset, of course, is Gallister, just as he is Sunset.'

'I tell you that I'm not working for Gallister,' Chisholm said sharply, though dismay was running through him now in a cold wave. 'Get that idea out of your head. I'm quite likely to be working against him. In fact—' he hesitated, and faced the bitter fact that he had been made a fool of—'if I'd known that Hogarth had any connection with Sunset, I wouldn't have taken the case in the first place.'

'Sure, sure, we knew all that,' Dunning conceded, unruffled. 'But don't get riled, Chisholm. You did take it, and you did a good piece of work—for yourself as well as for us. If you'd gotten off on the wrong foot, as you started in to do, you'd have been finished in this country before you ever got started. Now you're in—and when you're in with Sunset, that leaves no halfway about it. We expect good work, but we pay for it, and at top hand prices.'

'Just what is your connection with Sunset?' Chisholm demanded bluntly.

'I'm foreman. Next to Gallister, what I say, goes.'

'And so you played me for a sucker, did
29

you?'

'Well, you can put it that way, if you like the sound of it.' Dunning grinned faintly and his calm was unshaken. 'The way I figure it is, we did you a good turn, and you did us one. I could find a lot nicer way to describe it than that.'

Chisholm was white-hot with fury, but he kept a tight leash on his temper.

'Take your money,' he rasped. 'I'm not working for Symes Gallister. Maybe I will, later—if he wants me to. And maybe not. I'll look into that more fully before I decide.'

Dunning made no move to touch the money, which fell to the floor.

'That's your fee for a job which you've already done, and for you to do with as you please.' He shrugged. 'But maybe I'd better wise you up a little. Like I say, that was a nice trick you pulled, and clever. But it don't make a bit of difference to the facts—not a damn bit of difference. Brick Hogarth is about as soft a spoken gent as you'd find anywhere, always polite and nice. But he's killed nine men that he admits to himself, and I wouldn't know how many more. And he killed that man yesterday, and plenty saw him do it.

'On top of that, he's Sunset's top gunslick—and everybody knows that, too. You took his case, and pulled a fast one, which was duly appreciated—but the jury would have turned him loose in any case. As it is, though, everybody, from the youngest bud to Grandma Bascom, knows that you're Symes Gallister's man now—and that means that you go along and do the legal work for Sunset.'

The true enormity of the thing was dawning on Chisholm now—not only how he had been tricked but the full extent of it. Gallister figured that he had circumvented him, so that he could not possibly help Mrs Gallister now. And he had come here with the notion of carrying the torch of justice high—of using law to further justice, and never for the circumventing of it.

'So you think that I'm a shyster, do you, Dunning?' he asked.

Tate Dunning crossed the room, and his face was serious, friendly.

'Chisholm,' he said, 'don't get me wrong. I reckon I know how you feel. But I have a job to do, and I do it. I learned a long while back that I couldn't make the world over, all by myself— and that nobody else gave a damn! You might as well get that into your head, too. I know you're no shyster but, just the same, you gave a right good imitation of one today. And what others see, they believe. You're working for Symes Gallister, like it or not. For it's him or nobody, after today. No decent folks around here would hire you to defend a dog!'

CHAPTER FIVE

Humiliation burned in Chisholm. The whole thing was clear enough to him now. Jud Rance had recognized the danger and had ridden on ahead, beating the stage, had reported to his bosses. And they had lost no time in taking action, moving deviously, playing him for a fool.

And he had been a fool. He had swallowed their bait, hook, line and sinker. Even though he had suspected a trap at the first, he had been lulled by the story which Dunning had told, and then, recklessly, without stopping to really investigate, he had plunged ahead.

His justification had been that he was thinking of Molly Gallister—or Molly Benton, as she still should be. He had wanted to help her, to be in a position where he could exert some influence, and this had seemed such a perfect opportunity. If he could take the case of an underdog, a man who seemed to have no chance at all, and win in a spectacular way, then people would know him, the court would have to listen to him.

That had been the notion in the back of his mind—a part of his old training, he realized. And it had all seemed to work well. Far too smoothly, he knew now, thinking back. He had been trapped and made a fool of, and now he was branded like a renegade steer—branded by Sunset.

It had been his intention to go to Molly without loss of time, but now he knew that he had to get off by himself, to think this thing over. He had meant exactly what he said, when he told Tate Dunning that he was not going to work for Symes Gallister. But now, when it was perhaps too late to matter, he would move carefully, warily, being sure of his ground before he advanced.

Like it or not, and he liked none of it, it seemed that Dunning was right. Chisholm could see it in the way men looked at him, as he came out on the street. There was not the respect in their eyes that he had hoped to see. They regarded his accomplishment as Dunning had done—in the light of a clever trick, a shyster trick. And while the majority here might be under the influence of Sunset, that did not make them respect a tricky lawyer.

He walked, with long, ground-pounding steps, to the livery stable and hired a horse. It would be like old times to be in the saddle again, and he had to get out, away from people.

With the town left behind, and riding to the west, it was a good enough land—better than to the eastward, and with room to breathe in. Only the water, when he tried it, was like that of Red Rock—brackish to the taste, unpleasant.

But here there were foothills, green-carpeted, with patches of trees and brush. His horse wanted to run, and that suited his own mood. Chisholm let it have its head, and they dashed across a meadow, swept up a slope in a gathering burst of speed, topped the crest, and were starting down when he saw the girl.

Here was a little, flowery slope, sun-kissed and pleasant, and she had left her own horse to its devices a little way off. She was sitting, skirts spread wide, daydreaming, totally unaware of him until his horse was almost upon her, even as he had not suspected that anyone would be within miles.

Chisholm pulled back sharply on the reins, bringing his cayuse to a sliding stop, hoofs braced and plowing the sod, scarcely a yard from her. He had a glimpse of a startled, up-turned face, of big blue eyes above a little, pertly up-tilted nose, with light, honey-colored hair in a wind-tossed cloud above.

For an instant her eyes met his own. And then, to his astonishment, she did not scream or jump to her feet in hasty and undignified and belated flight. Seeing that the horse had stopped and she was safe enough, the pallor in her cheeks was replaced by a returning bit of color; a smile turned up the corners of her mouth like opening rose petals. She sat there, quite unruffled, and smiled up at him.

'I'm sorry if I got in your way, Mr Chisholm,' she said demurely, 'but if you're not in too big a hurry—won't you stop a

34

while?'

Chisholm was off his horse then, far more flustered than the girl. He swept off his hat, anxiously.

'I'm sorry—I didn't know—I might have run you down—'

'But you didn't,' she reminded him, and he saw a dimple in one cheek for a moment. 'You showed very good horsemanship, and I assure you that I appreciate it.'

Chisholm caught some of her mood and dropped down on the grass himself. It had been a close thing but, since she chose to ignore it, he could do no less.

'I'll try and be less reckless in the future,' he promised. 'But you have the advantage of me. You seem to know who I am.'

'How could I help it, after this morning?' she asked.

Chisholm felt his face reddening.

'Were you there?' he asked. 'I didn't see you.'

'I was watching from the door of Father's office,' she explained. 'I'm Sandra Wood.'

'I'm very glad to know you, Miss Wood,' Chisholm agreed. 'I'm afraid that your father was rather put out with me.'

She shook her head, smilingly.

'Not at all,' she said. 'He likes men who have new ways of doing things.'

They talked for a while, then she prepared to ride back to town with him. Some of his depression lifted. Sandra, he discovered, had the gift of talking about impersonal things, of carefully keeping the conversation away from those matters which she sensed had depressed him. As they reached town again, Chisholm leaned forward.

'I haven't really apologized for nearly running over you,' he said, 'but you've been wonderful about it. I hope we may be friends.'

'I don't see why not,' she agreed. 'And if you're thinking of Dad, he will be no bar. I think you'll find, as you come to know him better, that he's rather a wonderful man.'

'I think that already—though my opinion of that trait in your family isn't confined to him,' Chisholm assured her, and saw the faint pulse of color in her cheeks as she rode on.

She had created a pleasant diversion, but she hadn't helped him to think. He was no nearer a solution of how next to proceed than he had been before. But his determination to go ahead, to live his own life in his own way, was unchanged.

Leaving his horse, he was passing the courthouse when the judge came out. Recognizing him, Wood waved cheerily, and they fell into step quite naturally.

'Sandra has just been telling me about you,' the judge said, his voice friendly. 'I hope that you won't allow the things which have happened today to upset you too much, sir. I gathered from something that she said that you were a little disturbed—which is natural, of course. But not all of us form ironclad opinions on the spur of the moment, you know.'

'I'm mighty glad that you feel that way about it, Judge,' Chisholm said fervently. 'I seem to have rather put my foot in it—but if the people of the community who really count will give me a chance, I think they'll find that my intentions are good.'

'I'm sure of it, sir—sure of it, on both counts,' Judge Wood assured him heartily. 'Er—older heads, I might say, and men with more experience of this particular community, have been fooled by some of the methods used against them, at times. And, er—I take it that you haven't personally met Mr Gallister?'

'No, I haven't.'

'Then you might as well do it now—nothing like knowing who you're dealing with. And he's coming here now.'

Chisholm's interest quickened. The man who was approaching them, his high-heeled boots making a quick, light clatter on the wooden sidewalk, was a striking figure of a man. Unlike Chisholm, he would be outstanding anywhere, under almost any circumstances.

He was not tall—scarcely more so than Chisholm, and, like him, he was rather slender in build. But there was a quick, alert poise about him which reminded Chisholm of a stalking cat—that trick of being able to put its feet down lightly, surely, without once

37

removing its eyes from the prey which it crept upon.

Symes Gallister had that easy, alert sureness. He was handsome, in an engaging sort of way, with heavy, bushy brows above a nose a bit too big, but these added to his appearance, instead of detracting, giving force to his face. Eyes so light blue that they were steely, under light-brown hair. But it was the personality of the man, an emanation which you could almost feel, that really set him apart. And then the judge was speaking. 'I think that you two gentlemen ought to meet each other.' He smiled. 'Symes, this is our new barrister, Mr Chisholm. Mr Chisholm, Mr Gallister.'

Gallister held out his hand, smiling warmly.

'I've been wanting to meet you, Mr Chisholm,' he declared. 'More particularly since I hear that there are grounds for misunderstanding between us. I'm sure that can all be cleared up.'

'That's the way I like to see things settled—out of court.' Judge Wood chuckled. 'Enables me to lead a lazier sort of existence. If you gentlemen will excuse me—'

He moved on and, after a momentary hesitation, Chisholm accepted the handshake, since he could not well refuse. But he had an unpleasant foreboding that plenty of people were watching that handclasp, here on the public street, and that if there had been any doubts in their minds about him before, there would be none now.

Yet Symes Gallister was not at all the sort of man that he had pictured him as being. Now he was looking at Chisholm with those heavy brows raised in an inquiring smile.

'You name the place, Chisholm,' he suggested, 'where we can talk. I'd like to have you come out to Sunset and spend the night. Or we can go somewhere here, if you prefer.'

'Somewhere here would be better, I think,' Chisholm said, a little tightly.

'Fine.' Gallister turned, led the way. 'There's a room here in The Saddle where we won't be disturbed.'

The Saddle was the big saloon opposite The Last Chance. Gallister led the way through it to a side room, comfortably furnished with a desk and deeply upholstered chairs. He raised his brows inquiringly again.

'Will you have something to drink?'

'Nothing, thanks,' Chisholm said shortly.

'Fine. You'll excuse me if I take a little, though—I like a spot of whisky at this time of day.' Gallister poured himself a stiff drink and tossed it off at a gulp, with as little apparent effect as if it had been water. He leaned back and crossed his legs, pausing momentarily to eye admiringly the gold-plated spur on his boot—a vicious-looking rowel if he had ever seen one, Chisholm thought.

'I've been talking to Dunning,' Gallister observed, 'and the trouble between us, as I see it, boils down to two things. One is the question of my wife. We'll take that up second, if you don't mind. The other is the trick—as I imagine you regard it—that Tate played on you, in regard to Brick.'

'That's about it,' Chisholm agreed.

'Tate Dunning is a mighty good man,' Gallister said slowly. 'I met him at Cornell—in fact, we were room-mates. He eased me over some of the rough spots—I was just a cowboy from the west, and a bit crude in spots, to start with. Tate was a playboy, with a millionaire father. Educated to expensive tastes, and then his old man had the bad taste to lose all his money and, to top that off, to blow his brains out. So Tate came back out this way with me. He fitted—and he's very loyal to my interests. But his methods, at times, are a bit like those which his father used to win a fortune in Wall Street, in the first place. Based on the notion that an ounce of prevention beats a carload of dead beef.'

Apparently feeling that that disposed of that question, and having thus neatly shouldered full responsibility for it on the shoulders of his foreman, Gallister turned abruptly to the other.

'As for Mrs Gallister—I'll have to confess that the subject is rather a sore spot, Mr Chisholm. I wouldn't even think of discussing it with most men. But since you are a lawyer, and she has, I believe, spoken to you in that capacity—well, that alters things, of course.'

Chisholm nodded, in silence.

'If you married a woman, believing that she loved you,' Gallister went on slowly, 'and then she turned against you immediately—refused to live with you, and, in short, suffered from delusions—well, frankly, what would you do? It isn't exactly a pleasant experience, and I may have made mistakes.' He shrugged and smiled. 'With me, it's a new experience. But I've tried to do the right thing, so far as I knew or have been advised. The doctors tell me that it's best to let her have her own way—within limits. They hope—and so do I—that, with a little patience, she will completely recover. But pending that time—well, she has to be watched over, guarded to a certain extent. I hope you appreciate that?'

'You remind me a lot of Tate Dunning,' Chisholm said dryly.

'How do you mean?' Color crept in Gallister's cheek, and, absently almost, he tossed off another drink.

'You both have a specious way of explaining things.'

'Then you don't believe me?'

'I'm afraid I don't. If what you say is true, then you shouldn't have any objections to my visiting your wife, as her lawyer. I promised her that I would. Maybe you won't believe this, but I'm no shyster. If I see any evidences that what you say is so, I'll try and convince her that

41

things are best as they are. But if I don't—then I'll try and see that she gets her rights, the same as any other American citizen.'

Raw anger reddened Gallister's cheeks for a moment, then seeped away, leaving them white. Only by that did he show it. His voice was level.

'I'm afraid that you're inclined to be a little headstrong, Chisholm,' he said. 'Don't you think so?'

'I'm remembering my promise to her—and the fact that Brick Hogarth is a gunman, a common killer—and in your employ.'

Gallister shrugged, and this time, still with no outward effect, he emptied the bottle.

'I'm sorry that we don't see eye to eye, Chisholm,' he said, and there seemed to be faint regret in his voice. 'I've tried my best— and so has Tate Dunning. All that I can do now is to warn you not to interfere.' Suddenly his voice was hard and ugly. 'Nobody, tenderfoot or otherwise, is going to bust up my plans!'

CHAPTER SIX

Without another word, Chisholm turned, left the room, and walked on out, through The Saddle. He was aware of covert glances which followed him as he went, but no one spoke to him or tried to stop him. But now he was cold and alert. If he had doubted before, that last

42

vestige of hesitation had been removed. Symes Gallister and his Sunset crew were dangerous, and the glimpse that he had had of the man's real nature gave him some inkling of the terror which seemed to dwell in Molly Benton's eyes when she thought of this man as a husband.

Here was something monstrous, he knew. Just what, he had yet to learn, but it was big, sinister. He had a suspicion that Judge Wood had preferred for him to see Symes Gallister and judge for himself—and that what he did now would be the real test, in the judge's eyes, if he went along with Gallister now, or if he stood on his own feet.

It was no light test. Men like the jurist might admire him if he made the right choice, but they were sadly in the minority hereabouts. Red Rock was Symes Gallister's town. The country was his country.

Only one thing was much different here than in the troubled land that he had known as a boy and young man. There, lawlessness had ridden roughshod, but the man who had dominated the country had been as rough and crude as the methods he used. The difference here was that Symes Gallister and his right-hand man were educated, polished. They could use indirect and subtle methods, such as had been tried against himself, to discredit him in the eyes of the community. But if those failed, they had the old-fashioned crew of gunmen to back them up.

And how far could he hope to get, working virtually alone, against such a combination? He had thought that, in getting an education, in trusting to law, he would have a powerful weapon against the conditions he had hated. But here he was faced with men who knew the use of subtle weapons as well as he did. He had virtually been warned to conform—or die. There could be no mistaking that last snarl of Gallister's.

On the street again, he hesitated for a moment. The sun was setting in a splash of color, off in the west. Long clouds stretched at right angles in either direction, bright with gold and crimson and all the other tints of the rainbow. There would be half an hour of twilight yet. Then the dark.

Abruptly, he turned, headed down the street and toward the little house on the outskirts where, he had learned, Molly Gallister lived with a combination housekeeper and companion. Maybe he was a fool, but he was going through with this. Men, at the last, had said that he had left one country because he had lost his nerve. That hadn't been true, but they had said it just the same. They wouldn't say the same thing here.

The house, he noted, was outwardly like many of the others—not too prepossessing. But it was set a little apart from its neighbors, and there were lace curtains at the windows, the scarlet flash of a geranium. These things set

44

it apart. A rather rickety porch went halfway around the house, on two sides. As he set foot on it, a lounging figure detached itself from the shadows at the corner and placed itself between him and the door. And this, Chisholm saw, was Jud Rance.

There was a scowl on Rance's face now, and he gave an ostentatious hitch to his gun-belt. Plainly, he had not forgotten the humiliation he had suffered at Chisholm's hands the day before, and just as plainly he was not in a forgiving mood.

'Better keep travelin', Chisholm,' he grunted. 'Right on down the road—an' out of town!'

'So it's to be direct action, this time?' Chisholm asked.

Rance eyed him challengingly.

'Anything you want,' he agreed.

'Don't you think that you're sort of overdoing this watchdog business?' Chisholm asked pleasantly. 'Everyone has certain rights in this country, you know.'

'I do as I'm told,' Rance said shortly. 'And a lot of lawyer words don't mean a damn thing to me.'

'So I judged. However, I came here to see Mrs Gallister, not you. So get out of the way.'

Rance did not move.

'I'm the only one you're seein' around here, Chisholm,' he warned. 'Yesterday, you kind of took me by surprise. But today, if you're wantin' trouble, I'll give you all you can use.'

From inside, Chisholm thought that he saw a curtain twitch a little. That meant that Molly Benton was in there, watching—and hoping that he would find a way to keep his promise. Since it was plain that he had to dispose of Rance first, he might as well be getting on with it.

Seeing the look in his eye, Rance was not disposed to wait. He lashed out suddenly, without warning, a pile-driver blow of a fist which had been calculated to pretty well end the fight before it had a chance to begin. But his eyes telegraphed his intention, and Chisholm twitched his head aside. Then, while Rance was still extended, off-balance, his own right hand shot out and closed on the gunman's collar.

With a twisting heave, Chisholm jerked him around and flung him clear off the porch—so heavily that Rance staggered and went to his knees, balancing for a moment on his hands before he came up again. By then, Chisholm was off the porch and beside him. He might have gone on into the house, but he was certain that Rance would follow him.

'If it's a fight that you're wanting, Rance, we'll have it here, and not on the porch,' he said pleasantly. 'Too hard on the house, that way.' And as Rance came to his feet, he hit him— such a blow as he had used the day before.

It drove Rance back, staggering him, but, as he had said, he was ready for it today. He swung, half bent over, and kicked out, and that blow was as treacherous a thing as Chisholm had ever encountered. Rance's heavy boot did not touch him, but the foot turned in a cunning slashing stroke. The sharp spur raked Chisholm's thigh, cutting savagely, drawing blood. The wheel of the spur caught, with a twist, in the torn cloth of his pants, and with a jerk, Rance not only had his spur loose again, but the twisting jerk took Chisholm off his feet, sent him sprawling.

Before he could recover, Rance was leaping at him with both feet in the air, the old lumberjack trick of smashing a man while he was down. But by now Chisholm knew what to expect, and he twisted aside, swept out an arm and wrapped it around Rance's legs as they thudded down almost beside his nose. With a savage jerk, he had the gunman upset on the ground.

Chisholm was up first, and again, as Rance came up, he hit him. This time it was another calculated blow, with all his skill and the driving force of his rage behind it, and it flung Rance back and down. His head hit the ground with a solid crack, and for a moment he lay there, arms wide flung, apparently with all the fight knocked out of him.

It had been short, but savage. Chisholm half turned toward the house, and it was a warning cry from the now partly opened window which swung him around again.

Rance was getting back on his feet. And this time, he had had enough of rough and tumble. The lesson of the day before he had regarded in the light of a fluke. But today he was convinced. Chisholm was too tough a hombre with his fists.

But Rance had been set here with a job to do, and whatever methods his employer might favor at times, he was always a disciple of direct action. Now he was dragging at his gun, his intention only too plain.

Chisholm knew then that he had just one chance. He was weaponless himself, and there was murder in Rance's distorted face. Chisholm leaped, and his fingers closed on Rance's wrist as the gun cleared leather. Then, locked together in deadly grapple, they struggled for possession of the gun.

Certain advantage lay with Rance. The gun was in his hand, and all that he had to do was to bring it to bear and squeeze the trigger. Chisholm, on the other hand, did not want to kill him. He wanted to get the gun away, but not to use it in turn. And though his own muscles were steely, Rance was bigger, and rock-hard as well.

They fought, straining, saying nothing. Chisholm had a feeling that many pairs of eyes were watching them—not alone from inside the house, but from other houses, from farther down the street. But it was only a feeling. No one else approached or made any move to interfere. This was Symes Gallister's town, and most men at least had learned their lesson.

The muzzle of the gun twisted a little, and he wrenched it away. Rance's face was beaded with sweat, Chisholm's own muscles seemed to crack. Rance lashed out with a savage kick, but again his eyes telegraphed his intention, and Chisholm threw himself aside in the nick of time, brought his whole weight swinging back with the leverage of his move, with Rance momentarily off-balance. It staggered Rance, and the gun almost came loose in Chisholm's twist.

Not quite. Rance was lowering his head, trying to close his teeth on Chisholm's wrist. Chisholm's elbow jerked and smashed against his nose, so that blood spurted. Rance cursed, and tried to butt, and blood sprayed over Chisholm, and again Rance put all his effort into turning the deadly muzzle of the gun against Chisholm's chest.

There was, Chisholm knew, a sheriff in this town. No one had told him whether the sheriff stood with Judge Wood for law and order, or whether he discreetly backed Symes Gallister. But the latter was more likely, since no one was coming to interfere here, and Rance's murderous intentions were clear enough to anyone who watched.

Despite all that he could do, the superior weight of the gunman was beginning to tell. A little more, and he'd be able to trigger.

Chisholm twisted again, with all the weight of his body, a cunning wrestling hold. It sent Rance off-balance, staggering, the gun slipped a little, and with renewed desperation they both struggled for possession.

There was a muffled report, and then the terrible pressure was relaxed, and Rance was limp, sagging in Chisholm's grip. As Chisholm jerked back, Rance sprawled headlong on the ground, the gun falling now at Chisholm's feet. And fresh blood was spouting—not from Rance's nose now, but from a small fountain which seemed to stem from just above his heart.

CHAPTER SEVEN

Dazed, wholly incredulous at the sudden grim jest of fate, Chisholm stared down at the sprawled figure of Rance. He had seen too many dead men, and he knew too well the location of the heart, to have any doubts. Rance was dead, with a bullet from his own gun through his heart. And it had been his own finger which had squeezed the trigger and sent it there.

The thing was one of those unchancy happenings, of course, which neither of them had been able to foresee. Rance had been grimly determined on killing Chisholm, and the moment had come when he was sure that the gun was pointing right. But in the same instant that he had squeezed the trigger, Chisholm's twist had jerked the gun around, and Rance had been unable to check that fatal pressure on the trigger.

Bloody, disheveled, breathless, Chisholm stared down. It had happened with such startling quickness as to take him as much by surprise as the gunman himself. His sole purpose had been to twist the gun away, then to use it to force Rance to quit; not to use it to kill with.

But the thing had happened. People would know which side he was on, now—if he lived to stay on any side long.

Now, at long last, he heard footsteps, and turned. The sun was gone, even the glory that had been in the west had faded to a drab blackness. But there was enough light left to gather and flash on the star which Sheriff Forbes wore as he came up.

He was a tall, weedy looking man, with clothes unpressed, soiled; and, seeing him at close range for the first time, the loose lips, the avid light in his eyes, Chisholm's earlier doubts were resolved, even before the sheriff spoke. A man like this would be a tool, at best. And in this country he would be, as naturally as breathing, a tool of the man who wielded power.

'Murdered him, have you?' he asked, his voice sharp and a little grating. He stooped for

51

a closer look. 'Shot right through the heart, looks like.'

'What do you mean, murdered?' Chisholm snapped testily. 'He was trying to kill me, and we were struggling for possession of the gun. It went off while he still had it.'

'That's a likely story,' the sheriff said sardonically, straightening and half turning, and now he had the gun in his hand. 'I saw the whole thing, comin' up the street. You was tryin' to bust in the house here, and he was tryin' to stop you. Then you shot him. Open an' shut case. So I'm placin' you under arrest. Better come peaceful.'

Sudden, brittle anger coursed in Chisholm. A cold-blooded effort had been made to murder him, and that was understandable. But what he had done now had been solely in self-defense, as could not but be readily apparent to anyone who had been watching, as the sheriff claimed to have been—though he had been very careful to keep back, not to interfere, so long as he had expected the gunman to win.

Only when it had unexpectedly gone against Rance was he taking a hand, and the crudeness of it, the manifest intention of Sunset—of Symes Gallister, working now through this tool of a sheriff—to charge Chisholm with murder, was too raw. There was nothing subtle here, but certainly it was vicious. Chisholm stepped back, his face going pale and cold. He had been put upon enough for one day.

'Sheriff,' he said, 'if you aren't a fool, you know very well that it was an accident. And that it wasn't my fault, but self-defense.'

Forbes spat.

'I saw it,' he reiterated. 'A right open-an'-shut case of cold-blooded murder. The evidence speaks for itself. Like I say, you're under arrest—'

He was still twiddling the gun on his finger, spinning it on the trigger-guard. Before he quite realized what was happening, Chisholm reached out and plucked it off, and had the butt resting against his own palm. It had been a long while since he had held a gun, and it gave him a strange sensation. He did not point it at the suddenly dumbfounded sheriff, but there was a solid, satisfying feeling to having it there.

'I'd think twice about that, if I were you, sheriff,' he said, and a drawl that had been long absent from his voice was back in it now. A sort of mocking note which surprised even himself. 'Happens I don't feel in the mood to be arrested—for murder. Not any.'

The sheriff looked at him sharply. This new note, the drawling, easy dialect, was not that of a rank tenderfoot but of an old hand on the range. And the way Chisholm handled that gun suggested the same thing.

One fact was notable. Despite a dead man lying there, and the certainty in Chisholm's mind that many a pair of eyes had witnessed the whole thing, no crowd was collecting, as was to have been expected. No one was coming near them. He had a sudden sinking sensation at the pit of his stomach. The killing of Rance had been accidental and unplanned, but what was happening now smacked of frame-up.

Which meant that no one would appear that he could claim as a witness in his own defense. But there would, of course, be plenty to make their appearance at the right moment to swear that it was as the sheriff had said, a cold-blooded killing, and that they too had been around to see all that. It was like an old, remembered picture, and the weapon of law and knowledge that he had thought to use against these things was suddenly only a shadow.

What details these witnesses would add for embellishment to their tale, even that he could recite as if from memory. But this was no memory of the past, but something happening to him now. Symes Gallister had warned him. He had flouted that warning, still strong in his conviction that law could be made to prevail. Now the machine which Gallister had built up was in operation, not to brush him aside, but to crush him.

There were two hopes. One was Molly. Chisholm was virtually certain that she, too, had witnessed the thing from inside the house. But in the next instant he knew that, even if she was allowed to get out of this house and to court, her testimony would be discredited

54

before she ever came to the witness stand.

Judge Wood was the other possibility. He was a fair jurist, judging by what Chisholm had seen. But the thing would be, after all, in the hands of a jury. And that was not too good.

'Better not add to yore offences by tryin' to resist arrest,' the sheriff warned ponderously, a little nervously. 'Won't do you no good. I'm the law—'

Someone else was finally coming, walking unhurriedly, but without hesitation as well, toward them. Chisholm drew a breath of relief as he recognized Judge Wood. The jurist looked concerned, a little troubled, but his face was friendly as he glanced from one to the other of them, then down to the dead man.

'What's this?' he asked. 'Has there been trouble of some sort? But I see that there has, of course.'

'This hombre tried to bust into the house there, an' Rance stopped him,' the sheriff explained. 'They fought, an' Chisholm killed Jud. I saw it. Cold-blooded murder. An' now he's tryin' to resist arrest.'

Now, as though the coming of the judge was a sort of shield for the rest of them, others were beginning to make their appearance, to collect. An uncommonly silent crowd, it seemed to Chisholm. He shrugged.

'If I'm refusing to be arrested, Judge, it's because I don't like to be framed,' he said bluntly. 'If the sheriff saw it, as he says he did, then he knows that he's lying when he claims it was murder. Rance was trying to kill me. I was trying to stop him. We struggled for possession of his gun, and somehow it went off, with the wholly regrettable result that you see. But it was self-defense, and Forbes knows it.'

Forbes, at this point, had the wit to say nothing. Judge Wood looked troubled.

'This is certainly an unfortunate occurrence,' he sighed. 'And the fact remains, much as we may all deplore it, that Rance is dead.' His voice took on a friendlier quality. 'Very likely Mr Forbes is confused as to what he saw, Chisholm. But he has his duty to perform, of course, and no choice on that point. And you, as an officer of the court and a student of the law, realize that fact. Also that there are certain formalities which must be observed. I don't want to give you advice. After all, this is rather shocking, and to you most of all, I am sure. But think of it calmly. You can't afford to get off on the wrong foot, at the very start of your career in this community. What I am trying to say is that it will be better if this is settled according to the due process of the law. It seems to me that it would be unfortunate to flout what you are here to defend, to have an unnecessary blemish against you.'

That was sensible, Chisholm realized, and it was friendly advice, offered in a friendly spirit. He glanced again at the sheriff, and knew that

56

the man was only a figurehead. If it came to a showdown, Chisholm knew that he could bluff him. Which was probably what the judge feared as well. Wood placed his hand on Chisholm's shoulder in friendly fashion.

'From what you say, the hearing will probably be only a formality,' he urged, 'but a necessary procedure, as you know so well. And in the meantime, I'm sure that bail can be arranged, if for any reason this drags out at all.'

It was that friendliness, the regard which he had come to feel for the judge, which decided Chisholm. For Judge Wood was right. And, since the hearing would be held before him, he was going as far as he possibly could now.

If Chisholm failed to clear this blemish against his reputation by legal means, then he would be finished here, as a lawyer, before he was well started. And for the other possible consequences of resisting arrest, or acting like a swaggering bravo—yes, certainly the judge was right.

'Thanks, Judge,' he agreed. 'I guess you're right about it. I'll go along with you, Sheriff.'

'That's showin' sense,' Forbes grunted. 'Otherwise I'd a had to shoot you.'

Chisholm clamped his lips on the retort which rose to them. Then he went with the sheriff, considerably relieved that the last part of it had worked out as it had. He knew that Sandra had spoken a good word for him to her father, and the judge was showing his friendship now. That made the needed difference, in such a situation.

And when it came to the hearing, he would show them again that he was a lawyer who understood what he was about—without the necessity of resorting to any trickery. When he was given a chance, he'd cross-question the sheriff. And with that official under oath, he'd make him wish that he had remained away from the scene a little longer—sufficiently so that he could not classify himself as a witness.

But when they entered the jail, passing first through the sheriff's untidy office, back down a dank, musty corridor with cells on either side, and the door of one of these had clanged shut behind him, there was something rather terrifyingly grim and final about it. Outside, it was growing quite dark by now, and the night was thick here, with nothing to relieve it. The stench was of a long unwashed place, strong, all-pervading. Something scurried in the gloom. A rat, Chisholm decided, and, eyes now accustomed to the dark, sank down on the edge of the bunk.

Promptly he stood up again. This was the sort of jail that he would expect a man like Forbes to keep. But it was different from the one he had been in when visiting Brick Hogarth, and now he understood why. This was a different jail—the county jail, of course. He had given no thought to it before, but it was apparent that Red Rock boasted both a town and a county jail. The other had a different man in charge.

There was a difference far greater than that between the two prisons, however. The one, where an employee of Sunset had been held, awaiting trial for murder, had been clean and relatively pleasant. This one crawled with vermin. The comparison, in his own mind, was not pleasant. Brick Hogarth, as he knew now, had been held only as a gesture, until they got ready to turn him loose. That he would be set free, had been a known thing to everyone but Chisholm. If it was to be only a formality in his case as well, why the difference now? An uneasy twinge troubled him, but he brushed it aside. Judge Wood would probably have him before him, for the hearing, within an hour.

He went to the little, high-up window and, by placing his hands on the bars, was able to stand on tiptoe and look out, on to a dingy, dark alley. Standing was tiresome, but it was preferable to even sitting on that bed.

There had been a light in the sheriff's office, but it had gone out now. He waited, hoping for something, conscious of growing hunger. But as the hours dragged and the town's lights winked out, one by one, it came to him that, not only was there to be no hearing that evening, as he had expected, but that he was to have no supper, either.

Disgusted, angry, he spent the longest night of his life. The other cells were all empty, he knew now—empty of men. Not of rats, mice and smaller vermin. The place swarmed with them. Bright, beady eyes winked at him from the gloom.

When the first faint light of day came creeping in, he was nearly exhausted from standing all night, but that was still preferable to sitting on that cot.

Another long hour dragged before Sheriff Forbes finally appeared, bringing his breakfast. It was a mess which ordinarily he would have scorned, but now the coffee was at least warming, and he was too hungry to be squeamish.

'What's the idea?' he demanded hotly. 'I thought I was supposed to be given a hearing, last evening.'

'What you think, an' what you get, 's two diff'rent things,' Forbes growled.

'Well, how long do I have to stay in this hog pen?' Chisholm insisted. 'I've got a few rights, as a citizen. I want a hearing, and soon.'

'Mighty anxious to make a trip to the gallers, ain't you?' the sheriff asked jeeringly.

'Gallows?' Chisholm repeated. 'Listen, Sheriff, you know good and well that you haven't the shadow of an excuse for holding me here. Rance was killed in self-defense—but I wasn't even responsible for that. I twisted the gun to keep him from shooting me—and he pulled the trigger on it himself.'

'That story ain't goin' to get you anywhere,'

Forbes retorted. 'Not any.'

'We'll see that at my hearing. When will it be?'

'I don't know nothin' about a hearin'. Yore trial will start in about an hour. An' tomorrow, at sunup, I'll be hangin' you. If you take a look out, it's light enough now so you can see the gallers.'

CHAPTER EIGHT

The judge's mood was a little heavy as he approached his own house, set a little back from the street, not far from the courthouse, and cheerfully bowered in vines and shrubs. Most of those were the work of Sandra, who was like her mother had been in that way. Green fingers, the judge reflected. He lifted his hand in courteous greeting to two or three acquaintances who called to him, and his walk was as dignified and unhurried as usual. But it was with a sense of relief that he noted the team of coal-black horses and the light carriage at the tie-post.

Helen Drummond was inside, as the team had made it clear that she would be. She was chattering like an excited magpie, and the similitude went farther—in the raven-black hair, the white sweater which she wore, with white driving gauntlets, and the pertly saucy face she turned to him as he entered.

61

'Hello, Judge. So glad to see you, just when I need reinforcements! I've been telling Sandra that she must come out to the ranch with me now for two or three days,' she announced brightly. 'I'm so lonesome out there that I stagnate, and besides, the change will do her good. I just won't take no!'

Sandra laughed a little.

'I'd love to go out to the Jigging J with you, of course, Helen,' she agreed, 'but I hate to go away and leave Dad all alone. He really needs someone to look after him.'

'If that's all that's worrying you, go right along,' the judge said briskly. 'I was just thinking the same, my dear—that a few days in the country would do you good. I'll be all right. Take her along, Helen, by all means.'

'I almost believe you want to get rid of me,' Sandra protested, as she got into her coat.

'Nonsense, my dear,' the judge returned smilingly. 'Never that.' But it would be a lot more convenient with her out of town for a couple of days. It was plain that she had not yet heard of this new affair concerning the lawyer, and this way, she would not hear of it until it had been resolved. That would be much better, for he had a notion that her sympathies were involved. It was with relief that he watched the blacks whirl away, with Helen Drummond's voice coming back like an unending refrain . . .

CHAPTER NINE

Chisholm's mood was anything but pleasant when he arrived at the courthouse. Unwashed, unshaven, dog-tired, and hustled along by the sheriff like any common felon, there was nothing reassuring when he entered the court itself. The jury box, which by rights should have stood empty, was filled now, and Judge Wood was on the bench, looking remote and austere. The bailiff called sharply for order, the charges were read, and the trial was under way with a clocklike smoothness, an oiled regularity and absence of ordinary form which was both startling and revealing.

If Chisholm had entertained any doubts after the long night, they were swiftly dispelled now. He had placed his trust in Judge Wood as a gentleman and an able jurist. But that, he saw, was only a front, like so much of the rest of it. Symes Gallister had a strange quirk in his nature, which was perhaps the result of his college training. He liked to do things with the appearance of legality, to go through the forms. But Red Rock was his town, and Chisholm knew now that Judge Wood was as much his man as was Sheriff Forbes. And today the form was being cut short, the whole procedure a mockery.

Chisholm was permitted to act as his own

attorney. But he had no witnesses to call, no chance to prepare his case. And this morning, as he had expected, there was a long array of witnesses who testified that they had seen the shooting, and who backed the sheriff's story. He was not permitted to question or to challenge any of the jurors.

And his cross-questioning of witnesses was cut short by objections of opposing counsel, which were invariably sustained. After a little, wearily, Chisholm turned to the bench.

'Judge,' he said, 'I am reminded of the parable of the man who went down to Jericho and fell among thieves. Last night, I was led to believe that there was a Good Samaritan present—but I see now that there are only the thieves. Under the circumstances, I see no purpose in going on with this mockery of a trial. If you are willing to give me a fair trial, before a fair-minded jury—'

The gavel crashed thunderously.

'Every pertinent fact seems now to be in possession of the jury,' Judge Wood said sharply, 'so you may retire to reach your verdict.'

The sheriff's hand was on Chisholm's shoulder, forcing him back. The foreman of the jury spat accurately toward the spittoon, looked around for a moment, and stood up.

'Ain't no need of us retirin', I reckon, Judge,' he said. 'Guess we're all agreed that he's guilty, ain't we, boys?'

There were nods and a chorus of agreement. And no dissenting voices. The foreman spat again, this time not so accurately.

'Looks like the best thing to do's to hang him,' he said, and led the way out of the box and out of the courtroom. Through the open door, Chisholm could see the twelve of them, heading without a break or hesitation for the nearest saloon.

Judge Wood stood up again, his eyes refusing to meet Chisholm's. His face flushed a little, then paled, but his voice was steady enough.

'In view of the verdict of the jury, I have no recourse but to sentence you to be hanged by the neck until dead—which sentence the sheriff will execute tomorrow at sunrise. Court is adjourned.'

He turned, almost stumbling with his haste, back into his own chambers. Chisholm watched him go, tight-lipped. He turned, and in that moment a pair of handcuffs clicked shut on his wrists. The sheriff smirked a little.

'Can't afford to take no chances with a des'prit character like you,' he said. 'Come along, now.'

Chisholm followed him, grimly silent. His illusions had been swept away, his beliefs shattered with swift and thorough precision. Judge Wood was a hypocrite, and he had used his position to betray Chisholm, both the evening before and now.

Rage was a tight thing in him, like the pressure of a blown-up paper bag, but there seemed no chance for it to find a vent. Forbes was taking no chances with him. Not until he had thrust him back into the same cell which he had occupied before did he unlock the fetters. Looking around now with new speculation, Chisholm saw that, whatever other defects this place might have, it was a thoroughly well-built jail. Even an expert at that sort of thing would have a tough time to break out of here, and he was no expert.

'I'm a fool,' he growled to himself. 'And they've played me for one, from start to finish! And now—they'll be hanging me in the morning! And this is your career, Chisholm—bringing the law to a lawless country!'

His thoughts shifted from himself to Molly Benton. She, too, had been caught in the net of Symes Gallister and was just as helpless against it. Her appeal to him had only gotten him into trouble, without helping her any. Curiously, he found that he did not resent his own predicament, in so far as she was concerned. She had been wholly innocent, at least, and she had probably expected that a man trained in the law would be able to at least look after himself. Chisholm smiled bitterly.

The worst of it was that he had let her down so completely. With himself, it would soon be over with. And under the circumstances, he had the feeling that hanging was preferable to

66

remaining alive and being a puppet of a man like Symes Gallister. How was the judge feeling now, he wondered, after the part he had played?

He toyed, grimly, with the notion of escaping. Prisoners sometimes feigned sickness or found other ways of fooling a sheriff and getting the upper hand. But he had a strong suspicion that Sheriff Forbes would not be easy to fool. Beyond removing the handcuffs, he had done nothing to improve the last hours of a man condemned to die. The cell here was just as vermin-ridden as before—more so, if anything.

Chisholm looked around it disgustedly. A few times, in the course of his legal training, he had visited jails, and some of them had been pretty bad. The indifference of the public to the condition of jails, where often boys and innocent men were held, was a shocking thing. But none of the places that he had seen had been so bad as this one. It didn't look as though this particular cell had been swept out or given any sort of cleaning for months—perhaps years.

There was debris in the corner under the cot, a pile of it which was disgusting to look at, as well as to the nose. A big rat scurried away from it, slipped through under the door, and out into the corridor. Few of these cells were even given much use, apparently, under the system of justice prevailing in Red Rock. So

Sheriff Forbes, acting as his own jailer, simply let things go.

Chisholm turned to staring out the window. Outside, there was fresh air and warming sunshine, though it was dank and fetid in here. He turned back at a scurrying noise to see the rat again. Disgustedly, he shoved the cot a little to the side and kicked viciously into the mass. The idea of a rat's nest in here!

Objects flew about, and he viewed them with increasing disgust. It looked as though an old coat had been torn and chewed into bits and woven through the mass of junk which the rat had packed here, an item at a time. There was an old shoe, part of an ancient hat. An egg, unbroken, but shiny and dark of shell. A big, rusty spike. A broken piece of mirror. A corroded two-bit piece. Torn pages from an old magazine. An empty forty-five shell.

Curiously now, Chisholm stirred what remained with his foot, while the rat blinked beady eyes at him from under the door, bold and resentful. Chisholm paid no attention to it, for now his breath was quickening with sudden excitement. Though it was dirty, almost slimy to the touch, he reached down now and picked up something from the far back corner of the pile, which was finally revealed.

All rats are pack rats, more or less, and this pile of loot had been long in accumulating, to judge by the sign. With such a slovenly, haphazard man as Sheriff Forbes in charge, nothing had been disturbed. And this thing, which had been brought, most likely, from the sheriff's office beyond the cell block, and had lain long forgotten, was a Colt's forty-five caliber revolver.

It was rusty, gummy, but when he tried it, it broke open, and inside, he saw with sharply indrawn breath, were six cartridges. Not empty shells, but the real thing.

Chisholm looked down at the rat, and for an instant it returned his stare, unwinkingly. Chisholm nodded gravely.

'Looks like I owe you an apology, Mr Rat,' he said. 'Maybe you didn't mean it that way, but you've been good for something just the same. I'll be getting out of here before long, and you can get on with your housekeeping again, so far as I'm concerned.'

Using the remains of the old cloth, he wiped the gun as clean as possible, and, slipping the shells out of the cylinder, twirled it several times. There had been nothing wrong with this gun when the rat had first brought it here. Probably the sheriff had taken it from some prisoner and had left it lying on a chair or on his desk in his office. The rat, always eager for fresh loot, attracted by the shiny look of it, had helped himself, dragging and carrying it back in here. And here it had remained, tucked in the bottom of that nest, long forgotten, apparently even by the rat.

It needed oiling and polishing rather badly,

but it would work now. Chisholm replaced the shells and slipped it into his coat pocket. Whatever happened, he had nothing to lose. And when the sheriff returned, he was going out of here—though maybe not in just the way that Sunset had planned for him.

CHAPTER TEN

It was getting warmer outside, the sun was getting around to his own window, high up and inadequate as it was. A thin shaft of gold penetrated and lay across the far wall, not reaching the floor. It showed the rusty, stained wall, and surprised some sort of a crawling bug which scurried away for a darker corner, not liking it at all. A fly buzzed in the window.

Outside, the town was very quiet. If anybody was shocked at the farce of a trial held this morning, or surprised at the outcome, it was evident that they were keeping it strictly to themselves, that they had no intention of saying or doing anything about it. Privately, a few of them might condemn Symes Gallister and the system in their own minds, but Chisholm was a perfect example of what happened to anyone rash enough to voice opposition aloud.

Across the street, and a little farther down, two saddled horses were tied, heads drooping in the sun. Chisholm eyed them and wished

70

that the sheriff would return, to bring him his
dinner—or for any reason, just so he would
come. Those horses could be very handy, if he
was outside now.

Nothing had broken the silence inside the
jail for hours, save the occasional noise of a
scurrying rat. His first excitement had worn
off, and Chisholm was tired again, legs aching
from standing for so long. But that verminous
cot was no more inviting than before. Even
standing was not a great deal better, in this
place. He felt that he needed a thorough
scrubbing and a change of clothes before he
would ever feel clean again. But, considering
the hidden merits of this system, he was not
disposed to kick too much about it.

Now, at long last, there was a stir in the
sheriff's office. Then he heard voices, and his
pulse quickened as he recognized one of them
as belonging to Molly Benton. Less and less
was he inclined to think of her as Mrs Symes
Gallister. Her voice was eager, pleading.

'But I just want to talk to him for a little
while, Sheriff. After all, what he did was for
me. And if he's to be hanged in the morning,
it's only fair that I should have a chance to talk
to him, to thank him.'

'I tell you, it's ag'in regulations, Mis'
Gallister,' Forbes replied.

'Regulations?' Molly repeated. 'You are
above regulations, Mr Forbes. Please!'

Evidently she was turning the charm of her

71

smile on him, for now he seemed to weaken a little.

'Well—mebby it won't do no harm, for just a minute,' he agreed. 'Come along, then.'

Chisholm saw them coming down the dusky corridor, saw the horror on Molly's face as she sniffed the stench of the place and looked around. But she said nothing about that, and there was a set look of determination on her face, of resolution, which Chisholm thought he understood. Apparently it was too plain, for Forbes saw it as well.

'You can talk with him through the bars,' he said. 'An' I'll stand back here an' keep an eye on things.'

'But can't I speak to him privately, Sheriff?' she pleaded. 'Won't—won't you let me in to see him?'

Forbes shook his head decisively.

'Nope. I know you pretty well, Miss Molly. Always up to some trick 'r other. Wouldn't surprise me none if you come here with some wild idee of tryin' to pull a gun on me and make me turn him loose. Anyway, I ain't takin' no chances. None whatever.'

Molly looked shocked and pained.

'Why, Sheriff! How could you think such a thing of me?'

'Easy enough,' he grunted. 'So, like I say, I ain't takin' no chances. I'm watchin' you every second. Try a trick, and I'll be ready for it. Now talk to him, if you feel like it.'

Molly looked at Forbes for a moment, some of the loathing which she felt creeping into her look. Chisholm was convinced now that she had come here with such a scheme in mind as the sheriff had imputed to her, and his heart warmed. But Forbes was keeping warily back, watching her, catlike. In his way, he was a shrewder, more efficient officer than Chisholm had given him credit for at first.

But he had overlooked one possibility, and that was the pack rat. With his attention on Molly, Forbes was paying no attention to Chisholm. But his thoughts were jerked roughly to him as Chisholm spoke.

'If you'll take a look, Sheriff, you'll see that I've got a gun—and that I've got you covered! And if *you* try a trick, I won't hesitate a split second to kill you. I feel in just the mood for it. Put up your hands—high!'

Sheriff Forbes stared, his jaw sagging as he saw the leveled muzzle of the gun. Then, slowly, he raised his arms.

'Wh-where'n tunket did you get a holt of a gun?' he gasped.

'Wouldn't you like to know?' Chisholm taunted. 'That's better. Get his gun, Molly—and the keys!'

Molly Benton had shot a quick, startled glance at Chisholm, as surprised by this turn of events as the sheriff himself. Now, sudden color blooming excitedly in her cheeks, she lost no time in obeying. As she took the sheriff's

73

gun, he tried to protest.

'You don't want to do a thing like that, Miss Molly. Makes you an accomplice of his'n, and that's—'

'And that's just what I want to be,' Molly said, and her voice was clipped and short, yet with a new, almost lilting note in it. 'Nothing could give me greater pleasure than to do this to you, Sheriff Forbes. I heard you last night— and heard how you perjured yourself to swear to a lie, to set a noose about the neck of an innocent man!'

She jabbed him suddenly in the back with the muzzle of his own gun, and the sheriff cringed. In her other hand, Molly now held the bunch of keys.

'Face the wall, there, and keep reaching,' she ordered, and Chisholm watched admiringly as, with swift assurance but no haste or waste motion, she tried the keys and found the one which fitted the cell door. As it swung open, she gestured to Forbes again.

'In you go,' she ordered. 'And I hope you enjoy some of your own filth!'

She locked the door again, turned to Chisholm, and, still without speaking directly to him, led the way down the corridor, ignoring the sudden frenzied pleas of the sheriff. At the end of the hall she locked the door there, and then they were in the office.

'There's another bunch of keys here somewhere,' she said. 'Let's find them. I want

74

to drop both bunches in the deepest pool of a creek, somewhere.'

Chisholm could understand how she felt. Likewise, it was a practical idea. With both doors locked, it would take quite a while to free the sheriff and delay pursuit just that much longer. With the same calm efficiency, she was pulling out drawers in the sheriff's desk, and now she brought to light the extra set of keys.

'I guess we're ready to go, now. Come on. I've got horses waiting right down the street here.'

'Do you know,' Chisholm said, 'you're rather wonderful!'

'The way you pulled that gun on him, from nowhere, was a nice trick itself,' Molly said, and she was smiling now. 'He was so suspicious that I wasn't sure just how I could fool him.'

'So you did come here with the idea of getting me out?'

'You're the only man who has dared stick up for me,' she said simply. 'I couldn't do any less for you, could I? Besides, I need a friend—we both do. Come on, now. We'll act as if we were just going about our business, and I don't believe anybody will notice.'

They came out into the sunlight and walked toward the horses which Chisholm had noticed before. Here, the street was virtually deserted. Not until they were in the saddle did anyone take a second look at them, and by then they were leaving town.

Chisholm felt an odd sense of exhilaration, of freedom. But he turned to her a little anxiously.

'I can't ever begin to thank you, for what you've done,' he said. 'But what are we going to do? I don't want to get you into any more trouble than you are already.'

'You couldn't,' she said serenely. 'And I don't believe I can get you into any worse trouble than I have already, either. So, as it's the two of us against the world, I think we should stick together, for a while at least.'

'You've got a plan?'

'Complete. As it happens, I own a ranch—the Trigger spread. That was one of the main reasons why Symes Gallister pretended to marry me, as I figure it—he wanted Trigger. It's not only one of the best ranches anywhere in this part of the country, but it has one great distinction. It's the only place anywhere in a hundred miles that has water that's fit to drink.'

'I've noticed that the water all around here is terrible,' Chisholm agreed.

Molly wrinkled her nose at him in a half smile.

'It's worse than that,' she said. 'It would and does corrode the insides of a copper kettle, to say nothing of a human stomach. But the water on Trigger is not only good, it's pure and sweet. When Symes Gallister married me—as he claims—about a month ago, he took over, fired

76

my crew, who were loyal to me, and installed his own crew. But my idea is to head for Trigger, right now. We'll get there, and between the two of us—and the element of surprise—I think we can take over again.'

The bigness and boldness of the idea appealed to Chisholm. This was something that the others would not be expecting, which would also be in its favor.

'How many in his crew there?' he asked.

'Be five or six, probably. Not too many. And while I'm not sure, I think Nellie may be there.'

'Nellie?'

'She goes with the place, as you might say. She's rather an institution, Nellie is. Housekeeper and cook. And if she's been allowed to stay, and lying low—well, she will be with us, that's one sure thing. What do you think of the idea?'

Chisholm grinned.

'I like it,' he confessed. 'Though, as to holding it, after they get organized again—'

'That may not be easy,' Molly conceded. 'But it will take a day or so for them to get ready. And my old crew are still hanging around the country. I think we can get them back in time for the fight—and there are five of them. Some of them are a little old, and none of them are gun-fighters, but they will fight as long as they can draw breath—for Trigger and me. How does it seem now?'

Chisholm drew a deep breath.

'Lead on, Molly MacDuff!' he said. 'This is getting interesting!'

CHAPTER ELEVEN

There was no pursuit. The thing had been well planned on Molly's part. The town was very quiet, without, as it happened, any of the crew of Sunset around. Some of Gallister's hangers-on were in the saloons; but, without the direction of their boss, or Tate Dunning, they did not amount to much. By the time they had discovered what had happened, and had freed the sheriff, then gotten word to Gallister, it would be night. There would be little that anyone could do before the next day.

And by that time, if all went well, they would be in possession of Trigger, with the old crew back. What would happen then was anybody's guess. If Symes Gallister tried to overwhelm them by sheer force of numbers, it might be done. But he was not apt to try that—not at first, at least. He was a master at indirection, as was Tate Dunning. Likewise, when he knew that Molly would be fighting shoulder to shoulder with the rest of her crew, against all invaders, Gallister was not apt to resort to violence.

Whether he loved his wife, or not, Chisholm seriously doubted. There was always that possibility, of course. And, if Molly had been

78

mentally a little off, his whole attitude and course of action could be pretty well explained and accounted for.

But from what he had seen of her, Chisholm was convinced that Molly was as sane and competent as anyone he had ever known. That was a part of Symes Gallister's fiction, his way of trying to get what he wanted, by indirection where he could not use straight action. And in its essence, it was as cheap and cowardly a trick, to impute insanity to the woman he claimed to have married, as anything that Chisholm had ever heard of.

So it seemed that what Gallister had wanted, even more than Molly herself, was Trigger. There was plenty that Chisholm did not yet know here, but the picture was beginning to take shape.

Molly turned to him, smiling again.

'I've gotten you into a lot of trouble—a really awful mess,' she said. 'But I'm not going to apologize or say that I'm sorry. I am sorry, of course—and then again I'm not! I know that you're a man, a real man, and you're fighting on my side! And you can't imagine how much better that makes me feel—like a caged bird that has escaped! I was beginning to be afraid that I would go crazy!'

'I don't wonder at that,' Chisholm agreed. 'How did it all happen, in the first place?'

She sobered.

'Symes Gallister has wanted Trigger for a

long time,' she explained, 'but for the last few months he has been more determined than ever to have it. He offered to buy, but we wouldn't sell—Dad and Jim and I. Jim was my brother. Then Dad died—he was thrown from his horse, out on the range, and—and his neck was broken. And then Jim—his horse fell on him. So—so Trigger belonged to me. I wouldn't sell, either. I love Trigger, and I love ranching,' she explained simply. 'Besides, it was home.'

'Of course.'

She flashed him a grateful look.

'Gallister proposed to me—several times. I always refused him. Then—then one day I woke up to be told that I was his wife. He insisted that we had been married that afternoon, by a regular preacher, and everything. All I know is that I drank some coffee in a little restaurant in another town, and then everything went fuzzy, and I didn't remember a thing more till there I was, that evening, on Sunset—with him telling me that we were married!'

She flushed hotly, remembering.

'He tried to kiss me, and I scratched him! Then I don't remember very well—my head was still rather fuzzy. But I got outside the house, and hid—with them searching for me, in the dark. Later, I got a horse, and rode back to Trigger—and almost walked into a trap. He was there, waiting for me—with his crew in control. But I heard them talking, and I turned and rode for town—with them chasing me!'

'The beasts!' Chisholm muttered.

'I owned that little house in town, and so I stayed there. He tried to persuade me to come back with him, but I refused. So he has made out to be very patient and understanding—and has made it look as if I was touched in the head, to act as I've done. He sent a big negress to be my housekeeper and companion—but really to be my jailer! Last night, I couldn't get out of the house to help you, because of her. She weighs two hundred, and is strong as a horse!'

'But you gave her the slip this afternoon?'

Molly smiled briefly.

'I found some of the knockout drops that they've used to put me to sleep two or three times, when they thought I had made plans to try and get away,' she explained, 'and I used those to turn the tables. Well, as I say, I've stayed there. I've tried to talk to Judge Wood, to get a lawyer to take my case, to get an annulment, a divorce—anything. But Red Rock is owned by Gallister. So is the law, everything. I've been well-treated, in a way, but absolutely helpless. I guess you know the rest.'

With what he had known and suspected already, the thing was not so surprising. And Symes Gallister had succeeded pretty well, by his appearance of a suffering husband exercising great forbearance, in winning most of the community over to thinking as he wanted them to think—that Molly Benton was

81

incompetent to do things for herself.

From what she had told him about the deaths of her father and brother, he suspected that there might have been foul play involved there. But that was something which it would be virtually impossible to prove now. Molly turned to him again.

'So you see why, being selfish, I'm glad to have gotten you into this! I certainly didn't want to get you into serious trouble—but you've demonstrated that you can put up a fight yourself. And now you're on my side! Now I've got an ally to fight with me, and for me. It's like Easter, and resurrection, and living again—after being buried alive!'

'I haven't shown up very brilliantly in any of this, so far,' Chisholm said, a little ruefully.

'You've been fooled, and imposed on,' Molly agreed. 'But that has happened to a lot of people. Symes Gallister is as smart as he is unscrupulous—and Tate Dunning is even more clever. But you're the first one to beat him this far—and we've just begun to fight!'

Chisholm drew a long breath.

'You're right there,' he agreed. 'We'll really have to scrap from here on out—and we'll sure do it!' He reflected soberly, aloud: 'I was so sure that the law, if it was handled right, given a chance, would be the solution—all the solution that was needed. I was dead wrong there.'

'Yes,' Molly agreed, 'you were—considering what we're up against in this community.
82

When the law, all the way down, gets taken over by crooks, then you have to use force against force to take it back again. But you have shown that you know how to fight, even if you are a lawyer.'

'I was raised as a cowboy,' Chisholm explained, reflecting thinly that the words did not tell a half of it. 'I'm not a tenderfoot.'

'I'm glad of that,' she exclaimed. 'I need somebody that knows ranching to help me run Trigger. You show better and better all the time.'

'I'm beginning to see that you're right about one thing.' Chisholm nodded. 'I made the mistake that a lot of people do—of thinking that because men had fought and died to win certain great rights, and to establish law and order, that those same processes could be kept and maintained of their own weight—without any more fighting. But it isn't that way. Abuses creep in, and evil men get control, even of the law. The great rights of mankind are kept only by fighting fresh battles every so often.'

'That sounds logical,' Molly agreed. 'It's like being strong and keeping fit. If you keep doing the right things, you stay strong. But if you quit, you get flabby and lose all that you had.' She pointed suddenly. 'There's Trigger. This is the edge of it. It's a couple of miles yet to the buildings. Maybe we'd better plan our campaign before we get there.'

The best way, they decided, would be to look

things over, then ride in and count on the element of surprise. It was growing dusk by now, and the night would be a cloak when they arrived. One good point was that the crew would likely all be back by then, so that there would be little danger of anyone else coming to bother them before the next day.

'I'm hoping that Nellie is still here,' Molly added. 'I haven't been able to find out whether she is or not. I know that she tried to get to see me, a few times, but she couldn't. If she's here, that will help.'

Now, in the soft glow of evening, set at the foot of a sprawling hill, they could see the buildings and corrals of Trigger. Cottonwood trees reached toward the darkening sky line, and it had a pleasant, kept-up appearance. They left their horses and went ahead on foot. From inside the house came a querulous voice, and Molly gripped Chisholm's arm.

'That's Nellie,' she said. 'She's still on the job!'

A towheaded cowboy came out from the house, rather hastily, and a roar of laughter went up from the group lounging by the bunkhouse. One man voiced the general thought.

'Ain't yore courtin' progressin' right, Rafe? Mebby you ain't got the proper technik.'

'That woman, she's hard to please.' Rafe grinned, and felt of his head. 'Durned if she didn't box my ears fer me!'

'Why, what was you tryin' to do? Kiss her?'

'Kiss her?' Rafe looked injured. 'I was only swipin' an extra hunk of peach pie.'

'Mebby she'd of liked it better if you'd a kissed her,' another man spoke up.

'Rafe's new,' Molly whispered. 'I never saw him before. But the others are all old Sunset hands. That man with the brown mustache and black hair is Pinto Lacey. He's foreman here, I expect—and he's bad. The fat one is Toothpicks—and he's dangerous, too. He always looks sleepy, but he isn't. Sam Bart has that droopy left eyelid—he got cut in a knife scrape, and it injured the muscle. And Shorty, with him there, is his sidekick. They're all tainted with the same stick.'

Shorty, at this juncture, yawned and stood up. It was a revealing sight, for he was all of six feet six and thin as a rail, with huge hands at the ends of very long arms.

'Think I'll go turn in,' he grunted. 'I'm sorter sleepy.'

'Wait a minute, Shorty!' Chisholm spoke from the corner of the bunkhouse, and his voice jarred the five of them to instant and strained attention. The lounging Pinto came to his feet, and all of them looked, watchfully and suspiciously, toward the lawyer, standing there, a few feet away. There was a gun-belt around his waist, but he had no weapon in his hand. After a moment, Toothpicks swore.

'Hell—it's the lawyer!'

85

'Yeah.' Pinto's eyes, a greenish-gray, narrowed dangerously. 'I thought they had you in jail, hombre?'

'They did,' Chisholm agreed. 'But I didn't like it.'

Silence dragged between them, while they eyed each other, warily. Shorty let go with a sudden cackle of laughter.

'You didn't like it,' he chortled. 'So yuh didn't stay, eh? That's a good one, danged if it ain't.'

'And I don't like you fellows here, either,' Chisholm went on. 'So you needn't stay!'

'Needn't stay? Say, what the blazes is this?' Pinto growled. 'What's goin' on?'

Molly stepped suddenly into sight.

'What is going on, is that I'm taking over Trigger again, Pinto Lacey!' she snapped. 'Mr Chisholm is foreman here now. And we don't want any Sunset men on this range. So you can pack your war bags and get off—and stay off!'

They stared at her in surprise for a moment, then back to Chisholm. A woman, and a lawyer. Contempt curled on Lacey's lips, but it was Toothpicks, the fat, sleepy-looking one, who made the move for his gun, showing a startling burst of speed.

But he checked the motion, half-completed, staring into the gun in Chisholm's hand, which was centered on his midriff. None of them had seen that gun get out of the holster and into his hand. It was more like a conjuring trick. Yet

86

there it was.

'Hold it, Toothpicks,' Chisholm warned, and his voice had a sudden steely quality to it. 'When a man has been sentenced to hang for a killer, the score isn't made any worse by doing some of the same!'

Before the menace of his weapon, the hands of the others raised, one by one—all except those of Rafe, who stared with sagging jaw. And at that juncture, Nellie appeared in the doorway behind them, cradling a rifle in the crook of her arm.

Nellie was tall, angular, and middle-aged, but with auburn hair which was still glossily beautiful. There was a competent look in her eye, not belied by her prompt action now.

'Praises be, you're back, Molly!' she said. 'And a man with you! Rafe, you lazy good-for-nothin', lift the hardware off'n them others!'

'Nellie!' Molly breathed. 'The same old Nellie! Is Rafe all right?'

'Aside from bein' bow-legged, homely, knock-kneed, lantern-jawed, lazy, no-count and always under foot, he ain't too bad,' Nellie granted, her sharp eyes never roving from the proceedings. 'Sure you got 'em all, Rafe? Take any guns in the bunkhouse, too.'

'I got ary weapon, I reckon, Nellie,' Rafe agreed.

'Then the rest of you no-good varmints get on your horses and git!' Nellie snapped, and waved the rifle menacingly. 'I been countin' the hours till this one! You ever show up here again, and I'll let 'leven diff'rent brands of daylight through the pack of you! Git!'

'We'll go,' Pinto promised, his voice tight. 'But we'll be comin' back!' His glance roved to Chisholm, shifted angrily to Rafe. 'We'll be rememberin' this, Rafe!'

'Ary one of you take a shot at Rafe, and I'll hunt you down and claw yore eyes out!' Nellie promised thinly. And then, the next instant, she had Molly in her arms and was crooning over her, soft-voiced and motherly.

CHAPTER TWELVE

Chisholm kept a wary eye on the others until he was sure they were gone, lost in the night. They would undoubtedly head for Sunset, but Sunset was a good way from here. Nellie was still exclaiming over Molly, like a hen with one chick.

'I've been that mad!' she exclaimed. 'I could have et nails and never knowed it! Three times I come to town and tried to see you, and they'd never let me! But we been makin' medicine here—gettin' ready to pull the trigger! Ain't that goin' off half-cocked to try and make a joke, though? And seems like you beat us to it and helped yourselves, instead.'

She looked keenly, approvingly, at Chisholm.

'You ain't one of these here handsome birds, all fine feathers and big crowin', that runs whenever a sparrer makes a shadder over the henyard.' She nodded. 'Deliver me from them!'

'What were you getting ready to do, Nellie?' Molly asked. 'Maybe it will fit in with our plans. For now that we've got Trigger back, we must hold on to it.'

'We'll hold it,' Nellie promised grimly. 'Them skunk-striped rannyhans won't come in here ag'in—'cept over my dead body. They took us by surprise the other time, but once is four times too many with them! What we was figgerin' on, Rafe and me—he snuk me that rifle, only this evenin'—was to get the old crew back and then sashay into town and bust things up—and get you out ag'in! We'd of done it, too, pretty quick—or showed them a mighty hot time of it.'

'I'll bet you would, Nellie. But where are the boys?'

'They been sort of pasturin' around like lost sheep. So we got word to them, and tonight they're to gather over to the old line cabin. Ought to be there now.'

'The line cabin!' Molly exclaimed excitedly. 'That's four miles north of here. It won't take long to get them here, now.'

'Shouldn't,' Nellie agreed. 'Rafe—where at is that lazy good-fer-nothin'? Oh, there you are, Rafe. You dust up there and bring 'em back with you, on the double-quick, now!'

'Yes'm, Nellie. I'm on my way,' Rafe agreed.

'Where did you pick up Rafe?' Molly asked, after he had gone.

'Didn't pick him up,' Nellie denied. 'He's like one of these here burrs on a horse's tail. Rough but clingin'. Seems like he struck the Sunset for a job, bein' iggerant of what a bunch of rattlesnakes them polecats was, anyway. They sent him over here, and the old fool went and got the notion he wanted to marry me!'

She giggled, suddenly and unexpectedly, and was herself again.

'Think of it! Wantin' to marry me!' She lowered her voice confidentially. 'At that, he ain't such a bad egg. No color to his hair, but kinda handy to have around. I saw where he could be useful, and he agreed. Been sorta acting as my go-ahead, as you might say. I guess I sure got him in bad with the rest of that crew, though.' She shook her head anxiously.

With the chance at hand, Chisholm lost no time, while Nellie was getting supper ready for them, in taking a bath and getting a change of clothes. These latter were provided by Molly, who explained that they had belonged to her brother. When Chisholm came out again, attired in blue denim shirt and chaps, he felt as if the transition back to his old life was complete. The law episode, studying and all the rest of it, was gone.

That had been a dream, he saw now—and the awakening from it had been violent. There was a place for such ordered law, and Molly was in need of a good lawyer, to obtain an annulment of her marriage to Gallister. But before a lawyer could function, the law itself must be purged, in this country—and that was a job which had to be carried through now. There could be no turning back, short of death.

'You folks want cawfee for supper?' Nellie called from the kitchen.

'Just water,' Molly answered from somewhere else. 'I've been dreaming of a drink of good water for the last month!'

Chisholm met her, at the kitchen door. Both of them stopped, and he was aware of the swift scrutiny, the look half of pleasure, half of sadness, in Molly's eyes.

'They fit you, don't they?' She nodded. 'I thought they would. And you look good in range togs.'

'I feel more like myself in them,' Chisholm confessed. He wanted to ask more about her brother, but this seemed hardly the time or place. Supper was ready, and they did full justice to it. And the water, pure and cold and sweet, was like nectar, after what he had been accustomed to for the last few days.

'With water like this, I'd think people would haul it to Red Rock to drink,' he said.

Nellie snorted.

'Most of them yahoos have drunk so much whisky they can't tell what they're drinkin', anyway,' she said sourly. 'An' half of them

91

ain't had a taste of water in years!'

With the meal tucked under his belt, and clean once more, Chisholm felt like a new man. In the kitchen, Nellie was singing, not unmusically, as she cleared away the dishes. Molly looked at Chisholm and smiled a little.

'Well?' she asked. 'What do we do next?'

'Sit tight, I think,' Chisholm decided, 'and see what happens. Then we can decide.'

'Maybe that's best,' she agreed. 'And it's good to be home again! But I'm worried about you. If Sheriff Forbes comes out here with a posse—'

'I'm betting that he won't,' Chisholm said confidently. 'Not here on Trigger. Gallister will tell him not to. Of course, if he ever catches me off of Trigger and has a good opportunity— that would be a different matter.'

'Maybe you're right,' Molly said thoughtfully. 'Gallister probably will want to handle things himself—everything considered. And the biggest thing to watch out for won't be a direct attack but a flanking movement.'

'I've had a few demonstrations of that,' Chisholm admitted, a little wryly. 'But I think I've had my eyes opened. For a long-range plan, what have you in mind?'

'Just to go ahead and run Trigger, the same as always. And if we have to fight to do it— we'll fight!'

That, it seemed to Chisholm, rather oversimplified it, but he was saved the need for an answer by the return of Rafe with the others of the old crew of Trigger. They came in, frankly pleased to be back and to see Molly again, and there were five of them. Good men, she insisted, so far as loyalty went, and the ability to run cattle was concerned. In a fight, such as was likely shaping up, their loyalty would be their biggest asset.

There was Big Foot Dalton, possessed of an enormous pair of feet and a thin, reedy voice; Silver, who was a little man of indefinite age and a ready smile; Swede and Dutch, two big, slow-moving, quiet men who seemed inseparable, and Andy, the old-timer of the bunch, who walked with a hobble and a lurch, due to some old foot injury.

'If we'd a known just what was goin' on, Miss Molly, we'd never a stood for it,' Silver declared, 'but they said you'd gone an' married that side-winder—an', well, we just couldn't get it figgered out for a spell.'

'That bane the way of it,' Swede conceded. 'They make big fools of us, by golly!'

'Yah! But not any more!' Dutch interjected.

'No, they aren't going to, any more,' Chisholm agreed. 'And that means that somebody has to stay awake and on guard, all the time. We can't have them slipping up and taking us by surprise.'

'I'll take the first watch, tonight,' Rafe offered, and looked sidewise at Nellie. 'Moon's comin' up,' he added with elaborate casualness.

'That'll be fine,' Chisholm agreed. 'You watch till midnight. Then you take the second watch, Dutch.'

He turned, stumbled off to bed. After standing all night the night before, and most of the day, he was played out, his legs almost numb with weariness. But when he awoke, with sunlight streaming in at the window and a meadow lark singing cheerfully somewhere outside, it seemed almost like a dream.

'I was supposed to have been stretching hemp, this morning,' he reflected. 'And they're going to be plenty peeved about this whole affair. Likely we'll have visitors pretty soon.'

But it was clear by now that Gallister was not going to rush things. The very deliberation with which he moved was far more terrifying than a swift and direct attack in force would have been. It showed that he had full confidence in his own power, in the ultimate outcome.

It was Andy who brought interesting news. He had been with Trigger since Molly Benton was a baby, and so spoke with the freedom of long association.

'Heard a piece of news in town, a day or so back,' he declared. 'Just got to thinkin' it over. Piece of business we ought to have.'

'What is it, Andy?' Molly asked.

'Gov'ment's going to buy beef for the Indians, a thousand head or so, from what I hear. Buy on sort of a contract basis. Well, Trigger's got that much beef that's just prime for marketin'. Ought to be a good thing. Not many outfits can fill such an order, right now.'

'It sounds worth while,' Molly agreed.

'Oughtn't to take us long to get a herd together, and have everything ready,' Andy pursued. 'And everybody knows the quality of Trigger beef. They—'

'How many'd you say?' Rafe demanded.

'A thousand head,' Andy explained. 'Why?' Rafe shook his head.

'Nothin',' he said. 'Only I was curious. I been here goin' on three weeks now, ridin' around this range most of the time. And I ain't seen more'n two-three hundred head of Trigger-branded beef in all that time— includin' cows with calves.'

CHAPTER THIRTEEN

That was a jarring statement, on Rafe's part. But he stuck to it doggedly. He had not helped to move any cattle, since coming here. In fact, there had been very little works, except routine. But it was plain enough that the big herds which had ranged on Trigger had been moved, since Symes Gallister had taken over the running of it.

''Course,' Rafe explained carefully, 'there's a lot of cattle rangin' on Trigger, right now.

95

Fifteen hundred to two thousand head, easy, besides them wearin' the Trigger brand. But the others, they're all Sunset.'

Molly's lips tightened. It was clear enough that Gallister had done a lot of moving around, since taking control. To find their own cattle, and get them back again, might be a big job—especially with Sunset controlling all the rest of the range, and ready to object to any move which they might make off Trigger.

Watching her, Chisholm was confident of two things. There would be no backing down in what lay ahead. And she was as completely normal as any person he had ever known.

Nellie stuck her head in the doorway.

'There's somebody comin',' she announced laconically. 'Looks to me like the old boy himse'f!'

Not bothering to amplify that somewhat ambiguous statement, she retreated to the kitchen. By now, the lone horseman was close enough for them to recognize Symes Gallister. He rode jauntily, as though the notion that he might be unwelcome or among a hostile crowd had never entered his head. In a way, Chisholm had to admire him. It was no accident that Sunset was the dominating power in this country.

'You talk to him,' Molly said, tight-lipped. 'I don't want to see him—or talk to him.'

She went into another room, and Chisholm met Gallister on the porch. His greeting was

96

cheerful.

'Ah, good morning, Chisholm. I rather thought I'd find you here. Beautiful day, isn't it?'

'I'm appreciating it a lot more than seemed likely, yesterday,' Chisholm agreed.

Gallister smiled, and seated himself on the porch rail.

'I'm afraid that Forbes went off half-cocked, as usual,' he said. 'He has a way of doing that. And he got together a bunch of witnesses who are saloon hangers-on, who perjured themselves because he told them to. Oh, I'll admit what you know as well as I do—that they all thought they were doing what I would want done. Loyalty can be sadly misdirected, of course. And I was out of town for a day or so—just got back late last evening. Naturally, once I had heard the story of what had actually happened, I put a stop to it.'

Chisholm was a little startled. This, he recognized, was another oblique attack, but it was the last thing he had expected.

'Just what do you mean by that?' he asked.

'What I say. I went to Judge Wood—who of course had only presided, as his position requires—with Forbes and a couple of others. They admitted the truth, that it was a clear case of self-defense. The court records were altered, and you're clear. Maybe you've noticed that Forbes hasn't been after you—though he was breathing fire when I got there. They had just sawed him out of his own jail.'

'You mean that he doesn't want to arrest me any more?'

Gallister grinned.

'I wouldn't go that far,' he said. 'There's nothing he'd like better, if he could get a good chance, I imagine. But your record is clear. He won't molest you.'

'And just what do you expect in return for this?' Chisholm demanded bluntly.

'A good question. And I'll give you a straight answer. I've tried to show that I'm fair-minded, whether you believe it or not. In return, I'd like to be accorded the same treatment.'

Chisholm shrugged.

'I've always tried to be fair-minded, as you call it,' he agreed. 'Go right ahead.'

'Well, naturally, I'd like to see my wife.'

'She doesn't care to see you. And so far as the law is concerned, I seriously doubt if she ever was your wife, legally, at all.'

For a moment, there was an ugly light in Gallister's eyes, such as Chisholm had seen there once before, just before they had parted the last time. Then the ranch owner was smiling again.

'We don't see eye to eye on a lot of things, do we? But I think you will have to agree that I have done everything I could to show understanding and forbearance.'

'You've done everything you could to make

it look that way,' Chisholm agreed dryly. 'There's a difference.'

'You don't seem inclined to meet me halfway.'

'A branded calf is scared of the iron.'

'Well, after what you've gone through, I can see your viewpoint. I've told you that it wasn't what I wanted.' Gallister's face was sober. 'As man to man, I'd like to ask you a question. I love my wife. I want to make her happy. But how the devil can I go about it to do anything, when she won't even see me or talk to me?'

'You used the wrong methods to start with.'

'Maybe I did. Well, I mean it. I want to do the right thing.'

'Then you'll consent to an annulment.'

Gallister shrugged impatiently.

'If I do that, I lose her,' he said. 'Would you do that if you were in my boots?'

'You've lost her already,' Chisholm pointed out. 'In fact, you never had her.'

'Maybe you're right.' Gallister stroked his mustache thoughtfully. 'I wonder if it's too late to start all over again? I'd like to make her believe—and you—that I mean what I say. I'm willing to buy Trigger here, for any fair price— say twenty dollars an acre, which is every cent that it's worth. And along with that, I'll consent to the annulment. Then maybe I'll have a chance to start from scratch again.'

Chisholm had a momentary doubt. If this was acting, then Gallister was putting on a very

99

convincing demonstration. And the price was certainly fair, for any land in this country.

'She doesn't want to sell,' he said shortly.

'But I want to buy,' Gallister insisted. 'Damn it, man, I've got the power to take what I want, including Trigger—take it and hold it and not pay a cent. And other things the same. You know that.' He stood up abruptly. 'I'll lose my temper if I argue with you any longer. I've made a fair offer. Sell me Trigger at that price, and Molly gets her annulment.'

'Why not the annulment first?'

Gallister shook his head decisively.

'Nope. All that I'd get would be the short end of the deal. Nobody respects a fool. I'll get farther by bargaining, and it's a fair proposition. Take it or leave it.'

He turned, strode back to his horse, mounted, and rode away, still unhurried. Chisholm swung around to find Molly in the doorway.

'I heard it all,' she said, and some of his own puzzlement was reflected on her face. 'I don't understand it.'

'He's got me guessing,' Chisholm confessed. 'I can't quite figure it.'

'Twenty an acre is a good price,' Molly said soberly. 'More than a fair price. You could buy any ranch in this country for fifteen—a lot of them for ten or twelve. Of course, Trigger's worth more—but it sounds like a fair price.'

'And you say he's been wanting it a long

time?'

'Quite a while, yes.' She faced him questioningly. 'Do you think we should take it? It's home, of course—but there are other good ranches, in other parts of the country. With that price, we could buy somewhere else, and start again—'

Chisholm wondered if she meant that 'we' as it sounded to him, but he kept a tight rein on himself. For with that sale, of course, would go the annulment, and she would be free, then— the thought set his blood to rioting.

'That would mean all the difference in the world,' Molly added. 'No fight—and a new chance. This way, he's got control of the range, and there's no telling where our herd is, now. It's awfully long odds—and if a fight does start, he'll throw everything he's got against us.'

'That's what puzzles me,' Chisholm confessed. 'He's tried to make out, for the looks of the thing, that he loves you, wants you. I don't believe him. He wants Trigger. And he's willing to do anything to get it. That way, he'd have it. But even in a fight, he's not so sure.'

'I've about the same feeling,' Molly agreed. 'But even so, wouldn't it be the sensible thing? To have a chance to start clean and fresh—a real start—'

That was what tempted Chisholm. To have Molly free—he knew, now, that nothing else mattered quite so much to him. But he shook his head with sudden decision.

'There's nothing that I'd like better, if it was the right thing to do. But we know it isn't. No use of blinding ourselves to what we know. I'd be shot, one way or another, before I was ever allowed to leave here. You'd be caught the same way you are already. And there's some reason why he aims to have Trigger. I aim to find out why—and keep it away from him!'

Molly nodded, and now there was a sudden sparkle in her eyes.

'I know that's the right answer,' she agreed. 'It will mean a fight—but we'll give him all he wants!'

CHAPTER FOURTEEN

This thing of fighting in the dark was what worried Chisholm most. With so much going on, the advantage was all with Sunset, until he learned what the stakes were. At least, he could familiarize himself with Trigger without more delay.

'How about showing me around, Rafe?' he asked. 'Got a gun handy?'

Rafe nodded his towhead and grinned. 'Allers aim to pack a hunk of shootin' steel,' he admitted. 'Never know when it might come in needful.'

'Good.' Chisholm examined his own, the weapon which the sheriff had been packing up to the day before. Later on, when Forbes was likely to be in a more reasonable frame of mind, he would return it to him, but for the present he would use it. That other old gun, which had been hidden in the rat's nest and which he had used to bluff the sheriff with, would need polishing and oiling before it was in really usable condition.

'The rest of you boys stick close around the buildings here, today,' he instructed. 'If any of you need to go anywhere, ride two and two—never alone. And keep a sharp eye peeled.'

He turned his horse, following Rafe's lead, and Molly waved to him from a window of the house. Chisholm returned the gesture, feeling strangely boyish again. It was as though these last years of study and training had been swept away, almost as though they had never been. The feel of a gun in his hand gave him a strange, heady feeling—an almost forgotten thrill. But before he was through with this, his legal training should come in handy. Law and order had to return to this range. There could be no security, no real happiness, for Molly or any like her, until that had been done.

They were soon out of sight of the buildings, taking a different route than he had followed in coming out from town. Trigger looked like what Molly had proclaimed it, and Gallister had admitted it to be—a better than average range. Now and again they passed clumps of cattle, most of them with the Sunset brand on their right hips. Despite the herds, however, the grass was excellent.

There were many springs, and Rafe commented that the water in all of them was good. A few of them combined here to form a fair-sized creek, which flowed for two or three miles before spreading out and losing itself in the thirsty earth.

Chisholm's glance fixed on something else, a tiny gleaming thing which looked alien on this landscape. Then he saw another and another—a line of stakes, of fresh new lumber, running from northeast to southwest, set at regular intervals. Like a survey line.

'What are those for?' he asked.

'Railroad,' Rafe said promptly. 'A gang of surveyors run 'em, two-three weeks ago. I'm new, in this part of the country,' he added. 'But not as new as you, I guess. From what I hear, they've been talkin' about a railroad for years now and hopin' it would come. And while the news ain't leaked out too much, looks like it was comin' all right.'

'And it runs right across the middle of Trigger, eh?'

'Yep.' Rafe grinned. 'A lot of folks in Red Rock, they're goin' to be mighty disappointed. Been countin' on the tracks, and talkin' big about bein' a mee-trop'lis one of these days. When they find it don't come in miles of 'em, they're goin' to chaw nails.'

'About how far does it miss them?'

'All of ten miles, I reckon.' He leaned closer. 'I heard some of the talk, 'mong the surveyors. The idee seems to be to build a new town—here on Trigger. By golly,' he added, 'talk uh the devil!'

Chisholm looked up sharply. His first reaction was that Rafe was speaking of his former boss, but it was not Symes Gallister who was coming into sight, over a low hill, about a quarter of a mile away. Instead, there was a buggy, with the top down, drawn by a team of high-stepping, coal-black horses, with two passengers filling the single seat to overflowing. One of them was a tall, well-built man, with a full black beard and mustache, and he was driving the team expertly. He took slightly less than half of the seat in his own right, but what space he did not require was more than used up by his companion.

He was a short, wide man, with glossy black sideburns and a face otherwise smooth-shaven, and wearing a tall black hat. His little eyes, almost lost in the folds of cumbering flesh, were none the less very bright and quick. Though they were still some distance away, Rafe lowered his voice.

'They're from the railroad,' he said. 'Seen 'em before. Couple uh the bigwigs!'

The buggy was heading straight toward them now, the driver deftly negotiating such obstructions as were in the way, avoiding the more difficult places, since the springs already were pinched together and sagging dangerously on the one side. He pulled the team to a pawing, impatient stop, a few feet away, and nodded cheerfully.

'Hello, boys. Your boss anywhere around?'

Rafe removed his own faded, shapeless piece of headgear to scratch his head.

'Reckon likely you're referrin' to Gallister?' he asked cautiously.

'Exactly. Mr Symes Gallister.'

'Don't know just where he is, right now,' Rafe said. ''Cept that he ain't hereabouts—I hope! But if it's the boss yuh want to see, why—mebby you better talk to Mr Chisholm, here. He's runnin' Trigger, now.'

Both occupants of the buggy favored Chisholm with a more searching glance than before. The big man grunted, and the driver spoke quickly.

'Mr Chisholm, did you say? But I'm afraid I don't quite understand.'

'Chisholm is my name,' the latter admitted quietly. 'And I'm free to confess, gentlemen, that there's a lot which I don't understand, too. I'm new here. However, both as attorney and as acting foreman of this ranch, I represent the owner, Miss Molly Benton.'

The fat man's face did not change expression, but his companion looked puzzled.

'Miss Benton?' he repeated. 'I'm afraid I don't—but I beg your pardon. My name is Thomas—John Thomas. And this gentleman

106

is Mr Lang, superintendent of the Great Lakes and Pacific Railroad.'

Lang bobbed his chin a fraction of an inch.

'Glad to know you, Mr Chisholm. You'll pardon me—but I'm wedged in here till I can't stir—infernal instrument of torture, these things!'

'It's a pleasure to know you gentlemen,' Chisholm admitted.

'The same to you, Mr Chisholm. But there seems to be a misunderstanding somewhere. We have never heard of a Miss Benton, in connection with this place. All of our business has been with the owner—or so we understood—Mr Symes Gallister.'

'That doesn't surprise me,' Chisholm admitted. 'As I say, there's a lot that I don't understand, being new on the job here. In fact, until I saw this line of stakes a few minutes ago, I had never even heard of your intended railroad.'

'We've been trying to keep it as quiet as possible, until we had certain arrangements made. For perfectly good business reasons.'

'I understand. And you say that you have been dealing with Mr Gallister?'

'Yes. Isn't he the owner of Trigger, here?'

'Yes and no. About a month ago, he married Miss Molly Benton—or he claims that he did. Apparently the so-called wedding was fraudulent, and Miss Benton claims that it never took place at all. Following that,

107

however, Mr Gallister took over the running of Trigger, and, acting accordingly, has gone ahead as though he was the owner.'

Thomas looked puzzled.

'You say he claims to have married her? And she denies it? That has rather an extraordinary sound.'

'I know it does. And the whole thing hinges on that. If he had married her, he would, as her husband, probably have the right to look after her property. But since Miss Benton insists that there was no marriage in fact at all, and that the whole thing was fraudulent and done against her will, you can see the difference. She has never lived with him or admitted that he was her husband. And no longer ago than this morning, he practically admitted to me that, under the circumstances, an annulment was in order.'

Thomas frowned, and Lang looked interested.

'This grows more bewildering all the time,' Thomas objected. 'It's—to say the least—highly extraordinary!'

'You take the words right out of my mouth,' Chisholm said dryly. 'But that is the situation. And, things being as they are, we most certainly do not concede that Symes Gallister has any right to dispose of even a foot of Trigger land, or to make any arrangements whatsoever concerning it. Any deal will have to be made with Miss Benton.'

The two exchanged glances. Lang, unexpectedly, grinned.

'This is getting interesting,' he said.

'It sounds like the devil of a mess,' Thomas said sourly. 'You'll understand, Mr Chisholm, that I'm not doubting your word—I'm willing to be shown. But as it happens, we have already concluded a deal with Mr Gallister, which runs into a considerable cash sum—and you can see what that means.'

'I hope you haven't paid him the cash, yet,' Chisholm said.

'Not all of it, thank goodness. But we have contracted for a right of way across Trigger, for the use of its water, which is highly important, and for a townsite here on the ranch as well. Which all counts up.'

'Knowing Gallister, I imagine that he charged you plenty.'

Such of Thomas' face as was visible beyond his whiskers, darkened.

'Plenty!' he agreed. 'A hundred thousand dollars—besides a perpetual royalty on each gallon of water!'

Chisholm leaned forward in the saddle. Here, he knew, was the crux of the whole matter.

'And the whole thing hinges on the fact that you have to go through Trigger, because it's the only good water anywhere around?' he suggested.

'Exactly,' Lang agreed dryly. 'We were

running around in circles for a while. There's a five-hundred-mile stretch of country, all with water—if you can call it that—which would corrode any boiler ever made. And yet our locomotives must refill at least once in crossing that stretch. Then we found that there was good water on Trigger—the only decent water anywhere. It seemed like a lifesaver, until we got Gallister's terms. But we had no choice but to accept.'

It was clear enough to Chisholm now. Gallister had taken any means to get control of Trigger before the railroad came along, and, by that pseudo marriage, had managed it, then had made the deal. Knowing that the survey was coming close, and finding Molly adamant in her refusal either to sell to him or to marry him, he had tried strong-arm methods when time ran short.

And now, having made the deal, and received part of the down payment in cash, he was caught in a trap of his own setting. Small wonder that he had gone to such lengths to keep Molly from communicating with anyone outside of Red Rock, or most of all with Chisholm himself. When he had been unable to bribe or bluff him, he had set Jud Rance on guard, with orders to stop Chisholm or kill him. And when Jud had failed, the gallows, on a framed-up murder charge, had seemed the only safe way out of it.

Even that had failed. And so, desperate with

the knowledge that the railway officials would be back in these parts at any time, with the certainty that the secret could not much longer be kept, Gallister had played his part this morning, offering an annulment in exchange for Trigger—at what had sounded like a fair enough price then.

But, viewed in the light of these developments, it was no fair offer at all, but a gigantic swindle. Most of the money that he had offered to pay for the ranch would be returned to him by the railroad, and he would still own virtually all of the ranch, which, with a town built on it, and the railroad running straight through it, would automatically double in value overnight.

Nor was that all. A royalty on the water, which the railroad must use, year after year, would in the long run amount to a staggering sum in itself.

Lang squinted at Chisholm out of his little, shrewd eyes for a moment, went on: 'We've been perfectly frank with you, Mr Chisholm, and given you the full story. I trust that you won't try to take undue advantage of us on that account—though we've become rather accustomed to such treatment hereabouts,' he added grimly.

'We've been caught in a crotched stick,' Thomas added. 'But there's a limit to what our directors will stand for, or what our own judgment will accept.'

'I appreciate all that, gentlemen,' Chisholm said. 'As you say, it's a mess. I can promise you two things. We won't try to hold you up, or delay your operations in building the railroad, if you'll agree, once we have established proof of ownership, to give us equally good terms. And for the second, I think that I can safely say that Miss Benton won't want to hold you up for any such sum as you've already contracted for. A fair price, yes—but not highway robbery.'

The whiskers of Mr Thomas seemed to spread and relax a little, and the hidden twinkle in Lang's eyes was definite now.

'I thought that we were dealing with a man, for a change, John,' he said. 'We were right. We agree to your terms, Mr Chisholm—and I only hope that, when the thing is settled, we are dealing with you, rather than with Mr Gallister.'

'That goes double.' Thomas nodded. Then his lips set in a thin line. 'Right now, I guess we've got to find Gallister and have a little talk with him. One thing is sure. We've gone too far, with our present plans, to be stopped or turned back. Something has to be done.'

Nodding, he saluted with a wave of his whip, swung the impatient team, and the buggy started jouncing back the way it had come.

CHAPTER FIFTEEN

Chisholm watched them go, his thoughts beginning to clarify themselves. Now he had the explanation of what was back of all this, and it made a tremendous difference. The situation was no longer what it had been, that morning. Then, hard-pressed, but still aiming at his original goal, Gallister had been able to seem to afford to be generous. Buying Trigger would take a cut of the profits, where he had hoped, by making his marriage to Molly stick, to get it for nothing. But even that deal would be as good as he had originally hoped for, and it had been the expedient thing.

Now, however, the officials of the railroad would lose no time in seeing him, and they would bring pressure to bear. They were not like the others with whom Gallister had been dealing. They could not be murdered, if they refused to go along with him, nor bribed. And his bluff with them, while it had worked for holding them up, was played out now as well.

With others, he could order the sheriff to arrest them, confident that the law, as dealt out by hand-picked juries and administered by Judge Wood, would handle them efficiently. But that wouldn't work with the railroad, either. They would promptly take it to another court, a higher one, where Gallister's influence could not make itself felt. And, aired in such an atmosphere, Gallister could find himself in very hot water indeed.

Being no fool, he would know all of that, and know it soon. Which meant that he would be driven to take action. Chisholm did not fool himself with the thought that Gallister would withdraw as gracefully as he could, refunding the money that had already been paid to him, and sending the officials to make a new deal with Molly. That wasn't Symes Gallister's way.

Already, he had gone as far as attempted murder, and perhaps the real thing, to get his way. He was still, technically, and in this county, the husband of Molly Benton, and therefore legally entitled to make such deals as he chose in regard to Trigger. With that many aces in his hand, he wouldn't back down. He'd fight.

Rafe had sat, silent after the first interchange of greetings, listening with sagging jaw. Now he closed it and looked at Chisholm.

'Golly bullfrawgs!' he blurted. 'He ain't playin' for small spuds, is he? There'll be the devil to pay, now.'

'Sounds like it,' Chisholm agreed. He looked keenly at his companion. 'Scared, Rafe?'

Rafe shook his head vigorously.

'Hell, no,' he protested. Then a slow, uncertain smile played across his face. 'We-el, mebby that's puttin' it a mite too strong,' he

114

added. 'I guess I am scart—some. He's goin' to fight hard, now—and he ain't one to play gentle.'

'And they'll look on you as a traitor, since you drew Sunset pay for a spell. We'll need every good man we can get, Rafe. Just the same, if you'd rather not stay—'

This time, the shake of the head was decisive.

'I'm stayin',' Rafe said roughly. 'If they want a fight, they can have it. Sure I took his pay— but I earned it, doin' what I was hired for. An' I'd never of gone to him in the first place, for a job, if I'd knowed he was such a skunk. Besides,' he added, and the sheepish grin was in evidence again, 'you couldn't drag Nellie away with a log-chain an' four horses, an' as long as she's in it—we-el, I guess I'm stayin', too. Don't reckon she'll ever have no use for me—me bein' so gosh-danged homely, and all—still, that's the way it is.'

'Makes a pair of us,' Chisholm said, returning the grin. 'How much farther to the end of Trigger range?'

'Couple miles, this way. Want a look?'

'Guess we might as well. Better chance now than we'll have later, maybe. It'll take them the rest of the day to get over to Sunset and break the bad news.'

They jogged ahead and, though Trigger was a big spread, Chisholm was beginning, by now, to get a rough idea of what it was like. But one thing was becoming increasingly plain. Most

115

of the Trigger beef had been moved off the range, in the last month, and Sunset cattle brought to take their place.

Exactly where the significance of that came in, Chisholm wasn't sure. But that there was a good reason for it, in Gallister's mind, he had no doubt. It would, of course, give him that much better control of the outfit, which might have been the only reason.

Now, if they wanted to make a bid for supplying the Indians with beef, it was a hindrance. And the notion of bidding for that contract intrigued Chisholm. Few outfits, anywhere around here, could fill the order with a thousand head of prime beef. Sunset could do it, undoubtedly, but it wasn't likely that any other outfit could manage.

And since Trigger had the beef, and the price would be a good one, with the market ready to hand, it was more than worth while. He suspected that the books would be found to be in none too good shape. Trigger would need ready money, to keep operating. That might come from the railroad, but whether it did or not, it would be only good business to clinch this other deal if possible.

Such a sale, at top prices, would save a long drive out to market. And the cattle were ready for sale, this year. A year from now, it might be possible to ship by rail, saving all that drive. But that would be at least a year away. Right now, as foreman, he was interested in this other proposition.

He turned to Rafe.

'You any notion where the Trigger herd's been taken to, Rafe?' he asked.

Rafe removed his old hat, to run fingers through his tousled mop, disordering it still more.

'Like I said, there ain't been no more Trigger beef on this range, since I come, than there is now,' he explained. 'Still, I did hear some talk, a spell back—I got it! Pinto Lacey was talkin' to Sam Bart. Said somethin' about Trigger havin' a big herd over around Dry Creek.'

'Whereabouts is that?'

'I ain't never been there. Must be all of thirty miles from here, though. Over across the Rimrocks. Be a three-four day drive to get 'em back, out of that sort of country, if that's where they are.'

They exchanged glances, without comment. Both knew what that meant. If Gallister had had the Trigger herd moved off that far, there would be a lot more to getting it back than just the time and distance involved. Besides the difficulty of locating the cattle in the first place, there would be the crew of Sunset in between.

'Seems like he's been brewin' big medicine—an' a right nasty mess,' Rafe said thoughtfully. 'He—Golly Moses!'

They had just topped a long slope, from which it was possible to see for a considerable distance. Now, down ahead, not a quarter of a mile away, Chisholm saw, at the same instant, what had occasioned Rafe's startled comment.

Both of them had been confident that Gallister had returned home, following his visit to Trigger, and that it would still be a matter of hours before the railroad officials would find him to talk with him. But there, and seeing them at the same instant, heading their way already at a gallop, came Symes Gallister and three of his crew. Off about a mile, a receding speck in the distance, heading back toward town, was the buggy and span of blacks.

It was clear enough to Chisholm what had happened. Gallister must have gotten word, probably through some of his crew or willing henchmen from town, that Thomas and Lang were back and looking for him, driving out to Trigger. Realizing what that meant, Gallister had not bothered to return all the way home. With those of his crew whom he could readily pick up, he had ridden at all possible speed to intercept the railroaders before they got to the ranchhouse on Trigger—and had found them off there.

His hope, of course, had been to get to them before they could see Chisholm. But now he knew that he had been too late for that. Chance had played a part today, making a tear in the pattern. An error which could not have been foreseen. But Gallister was moving now, and fast, to rectify it.

'We better get back, fast,' Rafe gasped.

'They're sure lookin' for trouble!'

'Come on,' agreed Chisholm, and swung his horse. With odds of two to one, it was far better to run than to fight. For it wasn't often that Symes Gallister bothered to hire men at all, unless they were of the caliber of Jud Rance or Brick Hogarth—gunmen. But he had a feeling that Rafe wasn't of that class.

'You good with a gun?' he asked.

Rafe shook his head. 'Not ag'in that setup,' he said briefly. 'I sure wisht I was!'

Chisholm knew what he meant. Two of the three who rode with Gallister were Pinto Lacey and Toothpicks—the fat, slovenly looking puncher who was so fast and deadly in movement. Those two, as well as their boss, figured that they had a personal grudge against Rafe. And the fourth man had the look of belonging in such company.

The quartette was riding hard, coming in complete silence. That was understandable, for they preferred to be out of sight and sound of the unsuspecting railroad officials before anything happened, of course. But that twin purpose had already been accomplished. The four of them were sweeping over the rise where Chisholm and Rafe had been outlined only a short while before, and looking back, Chisholm saw that they had already shortened the distance a little. These were good horses, which he and Rafe rode—good, trustworthy cowponies.

But the others had horses selected for speed, and that speed was telling now. They were swinging a little, trying to head them, to keep them from getting back to the buildings on Trigger, where they might find help. Though, at this rate, and even if no shooting was indulged in, the superior speed of the others would catch them miles short of their goal.

Chisholm's hand half dropped to his gun, came away again. The range was still a little long for six-guns—and if it came to that, he'd have to make every bullet count.

CHAPTER SIXTEEN

The others were close enough, by now, that their faces could be seen, and the look on them. They were not trying to shoot, proof that they were confident of overtaking them in plenty of time. And that look on their faces told more than words could have done.

'We better shoot it out with 'em, hadn't we, boss?' Rafe asked, quietly. 'Make 'em shoot back, if we have to. I'd rather have it that way than have 'em get their hands on me.'

'Reckon you're right,' Chisholm agreed. 'But wait till they're close. It won't be all one-sided.'

He still had hopes of coming out of this alive. Neither his horse nor Rafe's had the speed of the others, but they were running hard and steady, and showing no undue signs of trouble. They had stamina and, if they were given a chance, could keep it up all the way back to the buildings. If they could once get in sight of them, the rest of the Trigger crew would come swarming out to turn the tables.

There was small chance of getting that close, though, in such a chase as this. But strategy might help. He spoke, low-voiced, to Rafe, swung his own horse suddenly to the left. It was a maneuver which would cost them a little more ground, but that was not the big point now. If they could get across into a cluster of small hills and buttes which reared not far off, there was always the chance of gaining something—or at least of being able to put up a better fight.

The suddenness of it had helped, and he saw that they would make it. His greatest handicap, Chisholm knew, was lack of knowledge of the country. If he knew it as well as the others did, it would help a lot. But there was more rough, broken country beyond. With luck, they might confuse their pursuers, get out of sight and gain ground.

He was drawing a deeper breath when two other riders appeared suddenly in their pathway, just in front of them—with drawn guns. Men on Sunset cayuses.

The surprise was complete. Chisholm realized, with bitter chagrin, that these two had been here all along, hoping that they would swing this way, or be turned. If not, they would be able to cut across from the flank, shortening the distance, lengthening the odds. Now it had worked out to a trap.

He grabbed toward his own gun, then regretfully checked the motion, pulling his horse to a stop with his other hand, lifting the one. Like Rafe, he'd been ready to make a fight of it, but with guns already upon them at point-blank range, it was suicide to resist now.

The other four were already pulling to a stop behind them, pocketing them. Gallister, his horse's hoofs plowing furrows as he slid to a stop, gave a short, clipped order.

'Get their guns, Sam!'

Sam Bart, he of the droopy left eyelid, one of the two who had surprised them, obeyed promptly. Gallister's face was stern and cold. Any of the easy friendliness of the other two occasions was gone now.

'Next, get down,' he ordered the two of them. 'We'll have you making no breaks, or trying it!'

Chisholm hesitated briefly, then obeyed. The breaks had been against them, today. Most of it was luck on the other side, Gallister and so many of his crew happening to be in the right places at the right time. But such things had a way of happening now and again. He'd seen such chains of events too many times to doubt. And you couldn't argue against facts.

Rafe was getting down, a little clumsily, his

122

face nearly as white as his hair, but otherwise he showed no sign of fear. Their captors were dismounting as well, surrounding them, and Chisholm, if he had had any doubts before, knew now that they were in for trouble.

Pinto Lacey had a wicked look in his eye. Having acted as Gallister's foreman on Trigger, he was a cut above the ordinary gunman, and now he showed it.

'I told you last night that we'd be comin' back, Rafe,' he said thinly. 'Remember?'

'I got a good memory,' Rafe conceded.

'Yeah? Didn't seem so, yesterday. Kind of forgot then, whose pay you was takin', didn't you?'

Rafe looked at him, but said nothing. They all knew, in fact, why he had acted as he had. Not particularly because he had anything against his former saddle-pards, or against Gallister and Sunset, but because Nellie was staying, and on the other side.

They knew it, but Rafe made no excuses. Like Chisholm, he realized that luck had played them a shabby trick, and that words here would be only a waste of breath.

Pinto hit him, suddenly, a quick jab which caught Rafe on the chin and jarred him. But he swung back angrily, only to be caught behind the ear by a gun barrel in the hands of Sam Bart. It slashed down, the sight slicing through the skin, bringing a spurt of blood behind it, half-dazing him.

123

Rafe staggered, almost went to his knees, and came up again by sheer effort of will. He tried to put up his hands, and his arms were leaden with the numbness crashing through his brain. Pinto hit him again, a series of cutting, brutal blows. Toothpicks would not be denied a share of the fun, and he swung a ponderous blow which came low, below the belt, and made Rafe retch and stagger, his face going white with agony.

Anger was a strong force in Chisholm, like steam lifting the lid of a teakettle. He knew that it was foolish, but he jumped suddenly, and the surprise of his movement got him away from the two who had been holding him. His own fist traveled a short, perfect line and connected on the jaw of Pinto Lacey just as he had hit Jud Rance back at Boxelder Creek. And with the same devastating effect. Pinto swayed and dropped, out cold.

But Chisholm had time for only the one blow. Before he could turn, Toothpicks and Bart were on him, dragging him back, holding both his arms, a third going to their assistance. He could not shake them off.

Gallister, smiling grimly, looked down at his fallen henchman, at the white and gasping Rafe, and coolly proceeded to roll himself a quirly.

'Take it easy, boys,' he cautioned, as they moved in at Rafe again. 'Wait till Pinto can take a hand. No hurry about this.'

He licked down the paper, stuck it between his lips and applied a match, flipping it away, expelling a gust of smoke. Then he looked at Chisholm and smiled a little.

'You've had a long string of luck, Chisholm,' he said. 'Longer than anybody else that's ever tried to buck me. And this morning, I made you a good offer. You sort of had me in a tight—then. When you didn't take it, your luck ran out.'

Chisholm shrugged.

'Speaking of luck,' he said, 'any string goes just so far, Gallister.'

'Yeah?' Gallister stomped the cigarette under his heel. 'Maybe you're right. But that's all you've had to operate on—luck. I don't trust to luck. I've got something a sight better—an organization that can't be beat.'

'Murder's a dangerous thing. And those railroaders are apt to ask questions.'

'Let them. They'll find no bullet holes in either of you. And accidents happen on the range. What's another one, more or less?'

Pinto Lacey was beginning to revive. He sat up, groggily, looked around, then, shaking his head, got uncertainly to his feet.

'Wh-what happened?' he asked.

'Nothing much,' Gallister said sardonically. 'Only the lawyer here, hit you—once!'

Pinto felt tenderly of his jaw. 'I'd rather be kicked by a mule,' he growled. But there was respect in his eyes as he looked at Chisholm.

'Damn, you don't act like no tenderfoot lawyer!'

'It's rather too bad that you didn't have sense enough to work with me,' Gallister said, and for just a moment there was some of the same admiration, almost a shade of regret, in his tone. 'We tried hard enough to get you started right.' His voice became coldly impersonal again. 'Had enough fun, Pinto?'

'Not yet,' Pinto grated. 'When I get through with this hombre, he'll know something's happened to him!'

Gallister shrugged.

'There's more important business,' he said. 'With these two out of the way, there won't be anything to worry about. This lawyer is the only one who is really dangerous.'

'How do we do it?' Pinto demanded. 'String 'em up?'

Gallister shook his head slowly, regretfully.

'I'd like that, but I'm afraid it wouldn't do. There's those railroaders, as he says. Something like that would be hard to explain.'

Pinto plucked at his mustache, his little eyes hard and glittering. 'I've got it,' he said. 'And it'll beat the other, at that.'

'What you got in mind?' Gallister asked.

'They need hangin',' Pinto went on, 'so tie their hands behind them, boys. Then a rope around their necks—and let them try runnin' behind horses a spell.'

Chisholm jerked violently, trying to break

free. But it was no good. Three were piling on each of them, himself and Rafe. Panting, their hands were tied behind their backs. There was a pleased, expectant light in the eyes of their captors.

'Fix the ropes,' Gallister ordered. 'Regular running nooses—those will beat the others. Tie the other ends to the saddle horns. Start at a trot—then gradually speed up!'

Already, a noose had been dropped over the head of Rafe, the other end of the rope tied to Pinto's saddle horn. Pinto swung on to his horse, and the other rope, Chisholm saw, was being fastened to Gallister's own saddle. In such a showdown as this, the innate savagery of the man was to the fore.

CHAPTER SEVENTEEN

Helen Drummond had long been one of Sandra Wood's best friends. They had gone to school together, and spending a night at the other's house had been an event during their young girlhood. It was still pleasant, but now it had a way of palling on Sandra within a few hours. For Helen, whatever her virtues, and they were many, was like the brook. She babbled, and she went on forever.

By nature, Sandra had grown quieter, more thoughtful, as she matured. Now, after two nights and a day of incessant talk, she was feeling a little smothered. For relief, the next morning, she lay long in bed, then turned with a sigh as she heard the irrepressible Helen come bounding up the stairs, two steps at a time. That meant that Helen was bursting with something more to talk about, and she came in like a whirlwind, to plump down on the bed beside her friend.

'Sandra! Guess what!' she gasped. 'Oh, it's the biggest news—about that new lawyer who's just come to town! They tried to hang him!'

'Hang him?' Sandra sat up with a jerk. 'Helen, what on earth are you talking about?'

'I hardly know,' Helen confessed. 'I'm so excited—oh, it's so thrilling and dreadful! He killed Jud Rance, and then he locked the sheriff up in his own jail and escaped, and—'

Gradually, little by little, Sandra got a coherent picture of what had happened in Red Rock since she had been away. One of the Jigging J cowboys had just returned, bringing the news. Helen made no understatement when she declared that she was excited.

'There he was in court, and your own father sentencing him to hang!' she ran on. 'And then he breaks jail and goes off with Symes Gallister's wife, out to her Trigger ranch, and kicks off the crew that was on it. And they say that the old Trigger crew is back—What are you going to do, Sandra?'

This last was occasioned by the somewhat

belated discovery that Sandra was out of bed and dressing with an almost frantic haste, and that her face was as white as the sheets.

'I've got to get in to town—get home,' Sandra said jerkily. 'You'll let me have a horse, won't you?'

'Why, of course,' Helen agreed, perplexed. 'A dozen, if you want them. But what's come over you, Sandra? What's the hurry? I was hoping that you'd stay at least until tomorrow—'

'I've got to go,' Sandra repeated, and she would offer no explanation. Helen could scarcely persuade her to wait even long enough to gulp a cup of coffee. That set, hurt look in Sandra's eyes puzzled and frightened her, but there was nothing that she could do about it. Then Sandra was away in a little cloud of dust, riding hard.

'She must be in love with him,' Helen decided. 'And yet, how could she? She's scarcely even seen him.'

For a while, Sandra rode hard, her thoughts in wild turmoil. Then, as she neared town, she slowed, first to a trot, then to a walk. Hurt and anger and resentment smoldered in her, but she dreaded what lay ahead. Still, it was not an issue which could be dodged, and in her forthright way she knew it.

Leaving the horse at a livery stable, she walked briskly to her home. Red Rock, today, seemed as undisturbed as ever. There was nothing about its outward look to indicate that, no longer ago than the previous morning, a man had been sentenced to hang here this morning—the sentence being pronounced by her own father. Sandra shivered a little. Nothing to indicate, either, that Chisholm had broken jail the evening before, riding casually out of town, leaving the sheriff locked in his own jail.

Today the sun shone as warmly as usual, though there was a faint haze in the air. Without giving it a conscious thought, Sandra realized that the long spell of good weather was drawing to a close. Storm lay somewhere, not far ahead. But it was already within her own heart as she pushed open the door.

Usually, at this hour of the day, her father would be in his rooms at the courthouse, busy with the duties of his office, and she had expected that he would be there now. Sight of him, sprawled laxly in a big chair, his face unshaven, hair disordered, eyes red, and with the strong odor of whisky about him, surprised and shocked her.

The judge sat up a little straighter, plainly as startled at seeing her now as she was at finding him here, and in such a condition. She could tell at a glance that he had been drinking, and she did not remember ever having seen him intoxicated before. Now he tried to pull himself together, and made a rather sorry job of it.

'Wh-why, hello, Shandra,' he said thickly.

'I—I didn't sphect—exsphect to shee—to see you home so—so soon.'

'Father!' Sandra exclaimed, aghast. 'You've been drinking! You're drunk!'

Slowly, unsteadily, the judge managed to get to his feet, clutching the back of the chair as he did so. His smile was wavery and uncertain. ''Fraid I—I did have a drop or so,' he managed carefully. 'I—I was short of—of upset—'

'I should think you would be!' And now the pent-up hurt and anger blazed out at him. 'Of all the cowardly, contemptible things to do! I wouldn't have believed it of you! To railroad an innocent man to the gallows, to make a mockery of his trial! I thought that you were an honest man, an upright and just judge!'

Before the bitter scorn in her voice, the judge quailed. He pulled himself a little straighter and made a pitiful attempt at dignity.

'Now, now, Shan—Sandra,' he managed. 'You mish—you misjudge me. I don't know what you're talkin'—talking 'bout—'

'You pretended to be his friend,' Sandra blazed at him again. 'Everybody knows that he was only defending himself when Jud Rance was trying to murder him! And that when he wasn't going to allow Forbes to arrest him for murder, that you assured him that it was only a formality! Plenty of people heard you say it, and it's all over the country now! And then the whole trial was a mockery, a farce—with him

131

railroaded straight to the gallows, when everyone knew that he was innocent!'

Suddenly she burst into tears, wild, uncontrollable weeping.

'Oh,' she gasped. 'I've always thought that you were so fine and honorable—and then you sell your soul to Symes Gallister, you do a thing like that—'

The judge stood, hesitant, sobered, uncertain of her and of himself. He took a step or so forward, and tried to reach out and pat her hand, and staggered again and all but fell. And the next instant, head upflung, she was eyeing him with scorn and loathing again.

'My own father!' she repeated. 'I wish I had died before this happened! Oh, Dad, how could you?'

She looked up at him, and he could find no answer. She saw the shame and humiliation in his face and turned suddenly toward the door. Something in her face penetrated to the judge's befuddled mind and shocked him. He took another step forward, crying out: 'Sandra! You don't understand! Where are you going? What are you going to do?'

From the doorway, she turned to look back for just an instant, and it seemed to him then that he was the condemned man in the dock, that she was the judge upon the bench, pronouncing sentence.

'I don't know,' she said bitterly. 'But I'm going away from here! Anywhere, or anything!

After what you've done—'

She did not finish it, only went on out and hurried down the walk to the gate and the street beyond. Hazily, uncertain, the judge watched her go. Once he made as if to call after her, then sighed and shook his head. He turned back, and his glance happened to fall on a half-empty flask of liquor. After a moment, almost fiercely now, he picked it up and drank it, scarcely blinking at the fiery potion. And then he collapsed again in his chair.

Almost mechanically, Sandra's steps took her back toward the livery stable. There she ordered her own horse saddled, still without any clear notion of what she was going to do or where she would go. Her mind was still shocked, more so than ever by the condition of her father. She had clutched at a straw of hope, as she rode in from the country, that somehow he would be able to explain. But sight of him drunk had crushed that last chance.

She was riding out of town when the solution came to her. This thing which had happened was monstrous, and she knew that a part of the responsibility for what had happened lay at her own door. She had talked with Tom Chisholm, and they had been friendly. She had told him, or what amounted to the same thing, that he could trust her father the judge. And she knew, instinctively, that it would be largely because of that assurance that he had trusted the judge, to his own betrayal.

'Probably he'll hate me, too,' she whispered to herself now. 'If he does, I can't blame him. But there's sure to be trouble, now—this is only just the beginning! Maybe I can help, a little.'

She rode steadily now, heading for Trigger. This was her own saddle pony, her own private saddle. Strapped to it was a leather case which she always carried as standard equipment when she rode. Now, on sudden impulse, she opened it, pulled out the small but powerful pair of silver-mounted field glasses. She raised them to her eyes and swept the horizon ahead, then steadied them suddenly.

With a little gasp, she took in what was happening, well off there at the side—so far away that none of them would see her. The field glasses brought all of the principal actors within her easy vision, and she recognized all of them but one. Six of them, including Gallister himself, were from Sunset, of course.

The other two seemed to be together in trouble, and one of them was Chisholm. She did not know the other man, and knew by that he must be new in this country as well. But he was with Chisholm, as was easy to tell, and both of them were prisoners. And from the brutal attack that Pinto Lacey was making on the other man, she was able to understand, as clearly as though they had explained it, what was in the wind.

The towheaded man was reeling, his face

134

bloody, crimson spattered on his hair as well. For the moment, Chisholm was only being held, but when he was allowed to witness such a thing, he would be sure to get some of it himself—or worse.

For a moment she watched, appalled and fascinated. What could she do to help, one against six? True, she carried a six-gun on the saddle, and she knew how to use it. But the others would see her long before she could get there, and she shivered at the thought.

Then it came to her, and the next instant she was spurring, desperately, on toward Trigger. If report was true, then the old crew of Trigger would likely be somewhere close to the ranchhouse now.

CHAPTER EIGHTEEN

Chisholm watched with tight lips. There was no need to appeal to this bunch for mercy, for while the element of personal revenge entered in, allowing long-suppressed savagery to come to the fore, still it was a matter of simple business in the long run. Here all sham and pretense had been stripped aside. If Chisholm lived, he knew enough to ruin Symes Gallister, to spoil all his plans. So he had to die, and Rafe with him—because Rafe too, happened to be here and likewise knew too much.

It was survival which counted, and so there

could be no halfway measures. Gallister and Pinto Lacey knew that, and the others who followed them. Here was none of the clutter of a courtroom, none of the befogging issues that civilized men like to throw about their deeds, to make them seem more excusable in their own eyes. Sunset knew it, and so did Trigger. In the last cold analysis it was simply a matter of business.

So any appeal would be wasted breath. There was just one chance, as Chisholm saw it, and that was a poor one, with the odds what they were. But it was better than nothing. Excitement coursed like heady wine in the veins of this Sunset crew now. For the moment they were like a wolf pack with fresh blood scent rank in their nostrils. Having gone this far, and having made up their minds to go wholly primitive in the show before them, they were enjoying it.

That excitement had made them careless in tying Chisholm's hands, though it was partly the fact that, even yet, they underestimated him. Always he looked inoffensive and rather helpless. He had cultivated that for a long while, and now it was useful again. Twisting, working silently, he had his wrists nearly loose. They were big wrists, made powerful by the boxing he had indulged in, that and other exercises. And his hands were small, graceful, not much larger than his wrists.

Now, with a steady pull, he had them free.

Pinto Lacey was just getting on his horse, looking triumphantly at Rafe. His eyes were blood-flecked, and the others were expectantly watching Rafe as well. Sam Bart, his droopy eyelid seeming to leer as he watched, stood just in front of Chisholm now. Toothpicks was behind Chisholm, but for the moment his attention too, was centered on Rafe.

Chisholm's fingers plucked the six-gun from Sam Bart's holster. Almost in the same motion, he raised it, then brought it swinging back and sidewise, in a calculated gesture which his boxing had taught him. The barrel cracked sharply against the heavy jaw of Toothpicks, and the fat man wavered on his feet, a stupid, hurt look spreading across his face for an instant. Then he dropped like a poleaxed steer.

The gun was up and ready now, and Chisholm did not hesitate. This was the primitive now, with survival itself as the stake. He fired, and Pinto Lacey leaned suddenly forward and slumped in the saddle, almost spilling out of it. His spooked cayuse snorted, but the reins had dropped from Pinto's lax fingers, on to the ground. Long trained to stand ground-hitched, the cayuse pranced a little, but it did not run, to jerk tight the noose running from saddle horn to the throat of Rafe.

There was cover not far off. Chisholm was running for it, and by the time he reached a big

137

rock and dropped behind it, the others had recovered from their surprise and had their own guns out. Chisholm had flung loose the noose from about his own neck as he started to run. Now he traded quick shots with Gallister; and then, recognizing how exposed were their own positions, the four remaining Sunset men were retreating, throwing back a rattle of lead as they did so, but looking for cover in turn.

Chisholm held his fire, for they had taken his gunbelt, and he had only four bullets left. Surprise had been on his side to begin with, but they would quickly recover and size that up as well as he did. Everything then was in their favor. They could use Rafe, still tied, still linked to the uneasy cayuse by the noose, and standing there helpless, as a hostage. Or they could spread out and come at him from all four sides at once, so that he would have no adequate cover. They had the horses, the numbers. And plenty of ammunition.

Four to one. Pretty soon, as Toothpicks recovered, it would be five to one.

His move had saved Rafe for the moment. But it looked to Chisholm as if he had just about played out his string. If he could get to the boogery cayuse and get Pinto's gun and belt, that would make a big difference. But he could no more cross that short strip of ground, in the teeth of a leaden hail, and live, than conjure cartridges out of the thin air. These four were gunmen.

Already, they were starting to pepper his rock with bullets, partly to keep him pinned down, partly to vent their sudden spleen for what had happened. Rafe stood there and looked unhappy.

Then the shooting stopped, and Gallister spoke, from where he had taken cover.

'Keep to cover and get back,' he ordered his men. 'Then spread out, so as to surround him. It's the quickest way.'

'Hell's bells,' Sam Bart exclaimed suddenly. 'Look there, boss!'

He pointed, and the others looked where he indicated. Still a long way off, but sweeping toward them over the horizon, came at least a half dozen riders, spurring hard. One look was enough to show that this was Trigger, riding to the rescue—and ready for a fight.

Gallister looked. And made up his mind instantly. 'We'll get out of here,' he decided. 'Fast!' He displayed his right to leadership then, swinging around.

'We prefer to hurry, Chisholm,' he said. 'Give us your word not to shoot at us, and we'll travel, and leave you alone. Take a shot at us, and we'll make a sieve of Rafe.'

'Fair enough,' Chisholm agreed. 'On your way. Take your fat friend, too.'

They did so, Gallister himself promptly stepping out into the open, shoving his gun back into the holster. Toothpicks was just starting to revive, and they boosted him into his saddle, then rode away. The others were getting almost within gunshot now, and Chisholm stepped into the open, waved to them, and crossed to free Rafe.

'Golly!' the latter breathed, as the noose was removed from about his throat and Chisholm untied his hands. 'I never want to wear a necktie ag'in! Not any sort.'

The others were coming up, now, the entire crew, it seemed, including Sandra Wood, Molly, and, just coming into sight, spurring wildly and flourishing a shotgun, Nellie herself. Swede looked stolidly at the scene, and nodded to Dutch.

'Ay tank we bane yoost a leetle late,' he decided.

Dutch nodded, gravely biting off a hunk of plug tobacco.

'Yah,' he agreed.

There were exclamations and explanations. Nellie was particularly vociferous and indignant, especially as she viewed the bedraggled appearance of Rafe. Andy winked solemnly at Silver.

'Kinda rough, mebby,' he said. 'But I reckon this ruckus has done Rafe more good with Nellie than all his courtin' has amounted to. Dang it, if he don't watch out, she'll go and marry him yet!'

They tied Pinto in his saddle, tied the reins up, and allowed the cayuse to follow the others toward Sunset. Some of the crew were

140

impatient to follow and press the fight, but Chisholm was equally eager to get back to Trigger without loss of time. It wasn't likely, but it might just occur to Gallister, given a little time, to swing around and beat them there. Once in possession of the buildings again, they wouldn't be easy to dislodge.

But they found everything as it had been left, and Sandra, dry-eyed now and tight-lipped, had explained why she had come out to Trigger today.

'I had to, Mr Chisholm,' she said. 'I know that I was partly responsible for your trusting my f-father. And—and I had been so sure that he was an honorable man—'

She stopped, biting her lips, and Chisholm saw that the tears were again very close to the surface.

'If you had anything to make up for, you've more than repaid the debt,' he assured her. 'We couldn't have held out much longer, the way things were. As for your father—I should have known, if I'd stopped to think, that he couldn't be judge here unless he was willing to do what Gallister wants done.'

'I suppose I should have seen that, too,' Sandra conceded soberly, 'but somehow I—I always thought that he—was different.'

'And you say that he—he had been drinking?' Molly asked.

'He was drunk,' Sandra said shortly.

'But I never knew that he drank any—'

141

'It's the first time that I ever knew it, either,' Sandra confessed miserably. 'Oh, I don't know what to do—only I can't stay there—not after he's done a thing like that—'

'You're more than welcome to stay here at Trigger, if you like, for as long as you like,' Molly assured her warmly. 'Though it may not be too good a place to stay—'

'You mean, because there's apt to be trouble?' Sandra demanded. 'Then I'm staying. They might hesitate a little longer to wage war, with me here too—since he is my father. But if it comes to fighting, I can shoot as well as anybody!'

'Don't be too hard on the judge,' Chisholm counseled. 'If he was drunk—well, it must have gone against the grain pretty badly, what he had to do. Maybe there's more to this than we know of.'

'I wish I could feel as good about it as you do,' Sandra said stormily. 'But I can't see that there could ever be any excuse for doing such a thing—betraying a man to death, after pretending to be your friend!'

Chisholm changed the subject. He explained now, this being the first opportunity, about the railroad and his meeting with the officials, and how, indirectly, that had led to the attack which Gallister and his men had made on them.

They were inside the house by now. Nellie was in the kitchen, caring for Rafe's hurts, too busy to invite herself to the council, Molly and Sandra both looked surprised.

'Red Rock is going to be awfully disappointed, about not getting the railroad, now that it is actually coming,' Sandra said. 'But a town here on Trigger, with good water, would be a whole lot better, of course.'

'But what will happen now?' Molly asked, practically. 'The secret is out, now. And they tried to kill you—'

'No telling what will happen next,' Chisholm conceded. 'But Gallister won't quit just because of a few setbacks. He's in this far too deeply for that. And he still holds plenty of trumps.'

'Such as?' Sandra asked.

'Technically—and legally enough for his operations—he is still your husband, Molly.'

Molly's face whitened a little.

'I'd fooled myself, today, into thinking there would be a way to get that annulment,' she said. 'But of course he won't give it—now.'

'No, not unless we meet his price,' Chisholm agreed. 'And I wouldn't recommend that.'

'He'll never get Trigger, now. Not if I can help it,' Molly said quietly.

'But with the railroad, this can be taken to another court, can't it?' Sandra asked, and flushed hotly at the thought.

'In the long run, yes,' Chisholm agreed. 'The point is that, right now, this will probably be settled in the court of Judge Colt—with hot lead. Before it ever has a chance to get to anything higher.'

They were all silent a moment, considering the implications of that. Gallister had shown, today as in the past, that he had no scruples in a fight. And the odds were heavily on his side.

'I just thought of something,' Sandra exclaimed with a start. 'Helen wedged it in this morning but, with the other that she had to tell, I didn't pay much attention to it at the time. But I think it's important.'

'What is it?' Molly asked.

'About your cattle—the Trigger herd,' Sandra explained. 'She said it was the talk in town that the government was buying a thousand head of Trigger beef for the Indians, and that the agent is to be in town today!'

'But I don't see—' Molly began, then stopped, her lips clamping. And from the light in her eyes, Chisholm saw that she did see.

'That probably means that Gallister's gone ahead and made the deal already.' He nodded. 'The same as with the railroad. He figured he had things under control.'

'But he can't do it, legally,' Molly cried. 'Everybody knows that I've never admitted that he was my husband—'

'He's already done a lot of things that didn't seem possible,' Chisholm pointed out, and stood up. 'If that agent is in town, I'll have to see him, let him understand just what the deal is.'

144

'Do you think that will stop it?' Sandra asked.

'We don't want to stop it,' Chisholm pointed out. 'It's a good deal, from all I can learn. What we want is to make sure that the money is paid to you, Molly, not to Sunset.'

'And you're a lawyer—you can make him understand about that,' Molly agreed. 'Oh— but I didn't think. You can't go to town. If you do, the sheriff will be after you again.'

'I've got to go,' Chisholm insisted. 'There's risk everywhere, now. If we take things lying down, we're licked. If we move fast and boldly and carry the war to the enemy, we may win. It's our only chance.'

'Then you'll have to take several men with you, to help out—'

Again, Chisholm shook his head.

'I'll take one,' he said. 'So far as force is concerned, they can outnumber us anyway. But the thing of first importance is to hold Trigger here. That means for you folks to stay here—all of you, all the time. And sit tight, no matter what happens. If they ever catch us off and get control here again, we're licked. But so long as you girls stay here, they can't get it, except by force—and I don't think they'll try that against you. Especially with the boys being handy with guns.'

'If you have to go, I suppose you have to go,' Molly agreed. 'But—promise me you'll be careful!'

'Careful,' said Chisholm, 'is my middle name. When I get in a fight, I like to finish it up!'

CHAPTER NINETEEN

Taking Andy with him, Chisholm rode for town. In a fight, as he realized, the oldster probably wouldn't be much good. But if it came to a fight, he'd need all of the Trigger crew behind him to make any appreciable difference against Sunset, and that wasn't possible.

So Andy would be a good man to have along. He was experienced, cool-headed, and that would count now for more than force. If it didn't—well, that was a risk that had to be run.

No one interfered with them as they rode in to town. Dusk was settling again, and the haze that had lain between the sun and the earth during the day was beginning to take on tangible shape and substance. The stars were shut away, and there was a feel of storm in the air. It might be delayed for a few hours, possibly even a couple of days. But it was on the way.

That suited Chisholm now. A dark night would be more to their advantage than the moon, which otherwise would have coursed the skies. Here in Red Rock he might have a few friends and well-wishers. But if so, most, and probably all, of them would keep discreetly silent and out of sight, their well-wishing confined to thought alone.

He left it to Andy to enter a saloon and buy a casual drink, and make even more casual inquiry. A quarter of an hour later, the old-timer rejoined him on a dark corner.

'Seems like yuh were right,' he said. 'This here agent for the gov'ment is in town, somewhere. Stayin' the night, I guess. Name of McQuade.'

'You didn't discover where he is?'

'Nope. Didn't want to appear too curious. Sort of got the idee, though, that he's sort of driftin' around—be in some saloon, likely.'

Chisholm nodded.

'We've got to find him,' he said, 'so we might as well be about it.'

He knew that their entrance into town had been observed. By now, the sheriff would have been informed. So there was no point to allowing Andy to make the rounds alone. If they wanted him, they would observe Andy and follow him, jumping them when Andy reported back. If there was to be anything of the sort, Chisholm preferred to have it out in the open, in the light, where he could have something to say about the method.

They went into the Saddle, and from the sudden tightness of the atmosphere, even before they had reached the bar, Chisholm knew that something was in the wind. He looked about carefully, but failed to see any punchers who looked like Sunset. Then, as he reached the bar, he understood. Sheriff Forbes was coming into the main part of the saloon from a side room.

He came through the door and paused there a moment, darting a quick, nervous glance about. That would mean, as Chisholm had expected, that he was not alone. The sheriff advanced again, halted with half the width of the room between them.

'Chisholm, I'm callin' on you to surrender peaceful,' he said. And his voice, try as he might, was a little strident and loud with nervousness.

'Going back to your stinking jail is the last thing I'll ever do,' Chisholm answered evenly, his own voice like a clear whisper in the silence. 'I didn't come to town looking for trouble, Forbes. But if you start anything, better be sure you can finish it!'

Forbes hesitated, and it was plain that he was uneasy. Men were moving back, getting out of the way if bullets should begin to fly, and the bartender had a wistful look of wishing that he was somewhere else. Andy had turned his back to Chisholm, was watching the door where they had entered.

'I'll keep an eye on this side of it, boss,' he said. 'You watch that way. I don't trust these jiggers half as far as a toad can hop.'

'Resistin' arrest ain't going to do you no

good,' Forbes said, not advancing. 'You cain't get away from a posse.'

'If I just go to jail to be hung, that's no better than killing you now, so far as I'm concerned,' Chisholm said. 'Fact is, I'd rather do it that way. Not that I want to kill you, Forbes. But it's up to you.'

Silence fell across the room. Forbes wet his lips and looked unhappy. But he had made his bluff and he dared not back down now. He took another step forward, and his hand half dropped toward his hip, and hesitated. Chisholm had not moved, but if Forbes had entertained any lingering doubts before, the easy watchfulness of the lawyer told him that Chisholm knew how to use a gun.

Unexpectedly, another voice cut across the tension.

'Hold it, feller,' Tate Dunning warned mildly. 'I figure this is between the two of 'em. Besides, I never did cotton to shootin' a man in the back—special when he was occupied otherwise.'

Chisholm resisted the impulse to turn his head, knowing that this might be a trick. But Andy, after a brief survey, reported: 'There's a kind of blind stair, off to the right there. Funny, I never noticed it before. And some hombre was sneakin' up there. Dunning, he spoiled that play.'

Silence held for a brief space, heavy and foreboding. Then Dunning spoke again from back in the shadows.

'He's vamoosed, gentlemen. There'll be no interference.'

It was that pronouncement which seemed to crack the sheriff's nerve. Quite plainly, this had been a trap set by him, with the other man posted to kill Chisholm while Forbes held his attention. Now that it had failed, and had been spoiled by Tate Dunning, whom of all men he had probably counted on to assist, if anything, Forbes lacked the courage to press it alone. It would be a shoot-out between himself and Chisholm, and fear of the outcome was a stark thing in Forbes' eyes now.

He stood for a moment, then wheeled, without looking back, tramped to the side door and through it, slamming it behind him with a thrust of his heel. Chisholm drew a long breath and turned to where Tate Dunning lounged, now in plain sight.

'Thanks, Dunning,' he said.

The foreman of Sunset smiled and shrugged.

'Don't get me wrong, Chisholm,' he murmured. 'We're on different sides of the fence. But you figured I pulled a fast one on you. Maybe I did. So that squares it now.'

Nodding, he turned, crossed to that same side door and went out. Chisholm wondered about him a little. Tate Dunning, they said, was wild, as bad as Gallister. To Chisholm, it seemed more likely that that wildness had put him in the power of Gallister.

After a moment, without ordering a drink, Chisholm went back to the front door, Andy beside him.

'That was close,' the old-timer said, once they were outside.

'Plenty,' Chisholm agreed. 'But I think it finishes it for tonight.'

'Mebby,' Andy conceded. 'Never can tell, though, with that kind. Forbes, he was a bushwacker 'fore Gallister ever put him in for sheriff. But he's afraid of Dunning.'

'Dunning has me puzzled,' Chisholm said.

'Reckon he's under Gallister's thumb,' Andy opined, backing Chisholm's own guess. 'But he frets at the bit considerable. And yuh spur him too hard, he rares up and bucks.'

The Last Chance was next. They went in, and there, lounging against the bar, was a man who Chisholm instinctively knew, must be the one they sought. Assurance, the stamp of officialdom, was upon him like a cloak. He was broad, not very tall, with a new Stetson on his head, and a big cigar clamped between thick lips. He had the look of a badly bored stranger, passing the time but not enjoying it. He turned at Chisholm's approach.

'Excuse me, but I'm looking for a man named McQuade,' Chisholm explained. 'Would you be him?'

The other man surveyed Chisholm briefly, flicked an eye toward Andy, and nodded, without much interest.

'That's my name,' he agreed.

'Then I'd like to talk to you—privately,' Chisholm suggested. 'Chisholm is my name. Lawyer—and acting foreman of Trigger.'

There was more interest in McQuade's glance now.

'I've no objections,' he said. 'Anything to pass the time. Shall we go to my room?'

Even in the room, McQuade did not remove his hat, and Chisholm guessed that, beneath it, he would reveal a totally bald head.

'Now,' McQuade asked, 'what's this all about?'

'I understand that you've made a deal to buy Trigger beef for the Indians,' Chisholm said, without preamble.

'Guess it's no secret. Anyway, if you're foreman there, you should know.'

'There's some things I don't know,' Chisholm said carefully. 'And some that you don't know either, I'm sure. As I told you, I'm a lawyer. I represent Molly Benton—who is supposed to be Mrs Symes Gallister. She is the actual owner of those cattle—and Symes Gallister has no right to sell them.'

'He's sold them to me, just the same.' McQuade shrugged. 'Forty dollars a head, to be paid on delivery. And if they're delivered, that's what counts.'

'Maybe. Let me explain.' Chisholm went on to outline the situation. McQuade listened without comment until he had finished, then flicked the ash from his cigar with a careless thumb.

'That's interesting,' he conceded, 'but I want those cattle. He's made the deal.'

'The deal suits us,' Chisholm said. 'But the money had better be paid to us—or you might find yourself in trouble.'

McQuade shrugged again.

'I'll let him worry about that, if he delivers the cattle,' he said. 'You can't come back on me, or the government, for fulfillin' our part of the contract. If Gallister's a crook, and steals cattle, there's a law to handle him.' He leaned forward. 'Tell you what. Those cattle are to be delivered to the reservation, in a week or less. You say the deal suits you. All right. You deliver 'em, with the authority you claim to have, and I'll pay the money to you. But if Gallister delivers 'em, I'll pay it to him. That's all I'm interested in—delivery. Goodnight gentlemen.'

CHAPTER TWENTY

Outside, the night had grown pitch black. The scattered lights of Red Rock seemed smaller against the enveloping gloom, like frightened sheep huddled together. In silence, they found their horses and rode out of town, and now there was a fine mistlike drizzle in the air.

'This'll be the line storm,' Andy opined

philosophically. 'Be a bad one, 'fore it's done with.'

Chisholm scarcely heard him. His mind was busy with what had transpired, with the problem of what lay ahead. There were certain definite things to be done, but when it came to the doing of them, he was up against a wall as blank as the darkness ahead. Nor could he see any light.

McQuade, he knew, meant just what he said. He had contracted for delivery of the cattle, and if they were turned in to the reservation at the proper time, it mattered little to him who brought them there, or who received the money, whether it was Symes Gallister or Mrs Symes Gallister. In either case, he would be well enough protected. Such matters had been handled far more loosely than that, plenty of times in the past.

Still with no solution in mind, they reached Trigger, soaked and tired. The storm was gradually thickening, with a little wind starting to run through it, the air was growing raw. No lights shone, and they sought their bunks, though Chisholm waited long enough to make sure that the guard was on duty. It was Dutch, tonight, vigilant but disgusted with the prospect.

'Ven a man ain't can see his face behind his hand,' as he expressed it. There was smoldering fire in the bunkhouse stove, and hot black coffee simmering in the pot.

154

At breakfast, Chisholm reported what he had learned during the evening. He passed over entirely his own brush with the sheriff.

'That's what we're up against now,' he summed up. 'Gallister has been playing both ends against the middle, with the notion of getting Trigger completely under his thumb. The herd, apparently, is off around Dry Creek, a day's ride from here. And then a job of rounding up, and three more days to get them to the reservation.'

'And he'll be sending his own crew to get them there,' Molly added thoughtfully, 'unless we beat them to it. And in either case, we'd be sure to clash with them.'

'That's the size of it,' Chisholm conceded.

'Let's call in the boys for a council of war,' Molly suggested, 'though I don't see how we're going to figure it out.'

Presently the others came in, gathering around a big stove which was glowing cheerfully this morning, in contrast to the coldly pelting rain outside. The storm was really hitting its stride now. Following a long dry spell, there was water everywhere, with mud underfoot, and the prospects, as Andy had predicted, of a bad one before it had spent itself.

Chisholm outlined the situation. There were a few moments of thoughtful silence, while men turned and squinted out into the storm, weighing the possibilities. Whatever had to be done, had to be done at once. Which meant traveling in disagreeable weather, to put it mildly. But it was Rafe who voiced the common thought.

'Be a lot easier to get there, in a storm like this, without runnin' into Sunset,' he said. 'Mebby that's the silver linin' to a right dark cloud.'

'Yeah,' Big Foot added ponderously. 'So we better get goin'.'

There was a chorus of approving nods. But Chisholm shook his head.

'You boys realize, I suppose, that we'd be running right into a fight, when we found the cattle?'

Again, there was the same slow, calculated nodding of heads. Swede spoke up.

'But us, we bane feel yoost like a scrap,' he explained.

'I wish it was that simple.' Chisholm sighed. 'It isn't. The herd is important—mighty important. So much so, that I don't intend to let them get away with it—not without putting up a fight, at least. But we can't afford to lose sight of the main issue. That happens to be Trigger itself, and the railroad. So long as we hold Trigger here, we've got an ace in the hole. If we move off with the whole crew, Sunset has plenty of men to throw a crew after the cattle, and another to come in here, too. Which means that you boys have to stay here and hold fast. It's far more important, of the two.'

'But if we stay here, they get the herd,' Andy pointed out. 'Can't get the beef without a crew. Even if Sunset wa'n't in the way at all, it takes a crew to round up a herd and drive it.'

'That's the trouble,' Chisholm confessed. 'We need two crews, and we've only got one. Any ideas?'

There was uneasy silence. Silver volunteered a half-hearted suggestion.

'We could mebby split up, half an' half.'

'That wouldn't do. Both crews would be too weak to do their job, and we'd lose out at both ends. No, there seems to be just one thing to do. I'll go over there today, with a bill of sale, properly made out and signed by you, Molly. That will give me one good point. And then I'll try and find a way to horn in—how, I don't know yet. But something may turn up. And it's the only way.'

Molly looked at him anxiously, started to say something, and bit her lip instead. Rafe voiced the thought.

'You'll just be pickin' a new place for yore funeral,' he sighed gloomily. 'They won't ask no better excuse than you hornin' in.'

'Have you any better suggestion?'

Again there was silence, while rain rattled gustily against the windows and made a steady drip from the eaves. Then, unexpectedly, Sandra spoke.

'I think I know a way to fix it,' she said, and colored a little as all eyes swung on her. But she went on, bravely enough. 'If you could hire a crew, over there—a good crew, that would solve it, wouldn't it?'

'It would sure help a lot,' Chisholm agreed. 'But who would work with us—especially against Sunset?'

'There's one outfit over there, the Seventy-nine,' Sandra went on. 'Bill Gordy runs it.'

'Yeah.' Andy nodded. 'I know Bill. A young feller, but a comer. And he don't love Sunset none. Just the same, a man'd be a fool to horn in on a proposition like this—'thout some mighty good reason.'

'I think I have the reason,' Sandra went on, though now her cheeks were pink. 'If—if you go to him and tell him that I—that I asked him to—I'm sure he'll do it. And his boys are nice boys, but a wild lot, always spoiling for trouble, and he keeps them on a pretty tight rein. If you offer them fighting men's pay for the job, they'll jump at the chance.'

Molly was looking at Sandra, a new light in her eyes.

'Isn't that asking a lot—of anyone?' she asked.

Sandra shook her head, her gaze on the floor.

'He's been wanting to marry me,' she said in a low voice. 'I—I haven't said yes. So he asked me to set him a task, something like ladies in olden times used to give their knights—he has a lot of romantic notions, that way. Give him something next to impossible to do. I told him that maybe I would.' Again she looked up, her eyes flashing.

'Well, this is it! Tell him the truth, Mr Chisholm. About—about me. About the name of Wood—how it has—has been dragged in the mud. If he doesn't want to have anything more to do with me, then, why that—that will be just fine. I'll understand. But if he does—well, then he's got to help me clear it. I don't know if you understand what I'm trying to say, but—but that's the way I feel—'

She was silent again, the pink fading to leave her face white again, the hurt raw in her voice. Almost on tiptoe, looking abashed, the crew went out, one by one. Molly had crossed to Sandra and was cradling her head in her own strong young arms.

'I think I understand, Sandra,' she said. 'And I—I think you're splendid. And I'm sure that Bill will jump at the chance! We'll give it to him, won't we?'

Chisholm nodded.

'Do no harm to ask, I guess,' he agreed. 'After we're through with Sunset, its name will fit better.'

Sandra tried to smile, through a mist of tears.

'That's what—what we all want,' she said. 'Sunset—has done this—to Dad. He never would have done what he did otherwise, I'm sure of that. And—and Symes Gallister—even

159

if he did pretend to marry you, Molly, he—he's pestered me, and—well, Bill Gordy hates him. And he'll ask nothing better than this chance! I'm sure of it.'

There was a moment of silence, broken now only by the steady drip of the rain and the slow tick-tock of a big clock in another room. It was strange, Chisholm reflected, how the tangled threads of a skein could come together, in a new and strange pattern—sometimes to weave a noose to hang a man. He stood up abruptly.

'I'll see he gets the chance,' he said. 'And I'll be startin', pronto.'

Rafe, from the kitchen, stuck his head in.

'I'll saddle the horses,' he said. 'Have 'em ready soon as you are.'

'One horse will be all I'm taking,' Chisholm said absently.

'Sure,' Rafe agreed. 'One for you, one for me.' He turned to duck back out, but Chisholm stopped him.

'One horse,' he repeated, 'for me. I ride alone.'

Rafe sighed, shook his head.

'Selfish,' he said. 'Some folks want to hawg all the fun. But of all I ever did see, you sure take the cake.'

CHAPTER TWENTY-ONE

Chisholm was under no delusions as to what lay ahead, as, slicker-wrapped, he was swallowed up by the storm. It was a blustery gale now, with the rain driving in sheets, and the slicker was little more than a gesture. He would soon be soaked to the skin, despite it. But the storm offered one real advantage. It was impossible to see for more than a few yards in any direction, and few men would be abroad on such a day unless driven by stern necessity, which offered him the best possible chance of getting through safely to Dry Creek and the 79 Ranch in the same vicinity. Despite the storm, he knew that he would have need of all his skill and luck to make it. Gallister would know what had happened in Red Rock last night. He was successful because of his ability to foresee most of the possible contingencies that might arise and his energy in moving to meet them.

So it was a foregone conclusion, in Chisholm's mind, that Gallister would figure that he, alone or perhaps with a part of the Trigger crew, would be trying to reach Dry Creek today. The odds would be heavy against Chisholm in any case, but Gallister was not the man to let it go at that. He'd have men strung across the line of travel, with the object of stopping Chisholm if he could.

Sunset had one big advantage in that their riders knew the country. But Chisholm had two. One was the storm, the other the chance of getting help from Bill Gordy and his 79. That was something which Gallister wouldn't be counting on.

The Rimrocks lay between. All of this was new country to Chisholm, but he knew in which direction to travel and about how far to go. And being in the saddle again was like old times. His sense of direction was excellent, and storm or night did not much affect it.

From what others had told him, he judged that the Rimrocks was a general term for a lot of rough country, a sort of divide, sloping gradually to a not very definite crest for several miles, then dropping away again in similar fashion. A rocky, broken stretch of country, largely treeless, save for a few scrub pine or juniper.

He could tell, as midday came on, that he was climbing. In the haze of storm it was not particularly apparent, but up here the air was colder, there was an occasional spit of snow woven with the rain. His horse, a buckskin, slipped and slid; for the ground was so soft now, even through the grass, as to be greasy. It made for slow going, and he was pretty thoroughly wet. But his six-gun, back under the slicker, was kept reasonably dry.

By now, he estimated that he had covered roughly half of the distance, and that he must

162

be close to the crest of the Rimrocks. Now and again a great boulder—some as large as claim shacks—would loom mistily through the storm. Little coulees, gashes in the landscape, would show, scantily fringed with thorn apple, wild currant, service berry. Small streams ran in most of them now, storm-born, destined to last only while it endured, brawling wildly in the madness of their brief existence.

Then, not far off, ghostly in the rain, he glimpsed someone, a man on a black horse. The rider happened to be sitting with his back turned to Chisholm, slicker turned up about his throat, hat pulled low and sodden. For the moment he was huddled there, his horse unmoving. And here, Chisholm guessed, was one of the watchers posted by Gallister. He had a good vantage point, where he could, under ordinary visual conditions, see for a long way in several directions. And here the natural landscape, with a bigger, canyonlike coulee off at the side to help, would send any rider heading just about as Chisholm had come.

He was about to swing his own cayuse and circle around, leaving the watcher undisturbed, when his horse kicked a loose stone. It rolled and bounded, making a sharp rattle against other rocks as it bounded down into the coulee. The watcher jerked around sharply.

For a moment, Chisholm stared, incredulous. His hand had twitched the slicker aside, was hovering close to his revolver, but he saw that the other man was making no hostile move, and then he recognized him. Silver. Riding a Trigger cayuse.

Silver recognized him at the same instant. His tense face relaxed a little, and he rode eagerly forward.

'Golly, boss,' he exclaimed. 'I thought I'd never find you in this rain. Ain't it a blinger?'

'What are you doing here?' Chisholm demanded.

Silver grinned uncertainly.

'Lookin' for you, I guess,' he said. 'After you'd gone, Miss Molly got plumb nervous. Figgered it'd be better if there was somebody to side you, somebody who knew the country. That was mainly why she picked on me, I guess. I been over every foot of it, times enough. Roundups and such. And that still leaves plenty of men to look after things, she said.'

'You must have ridden fast, to get here ahead of me.'

'Been travelin' pretty good, for a fact,' Silver agreed. 'Once or twice I cut your trail, then lost it ag'in. But knowin' the country, I thought I'd mebby meet up with you hereabouts. I was danged sure I could find you if the rain'd slack a little, so I could see.'

'You seem to have found me.' Chisholm's voice was thin. 'You say you know this country well?'

'Like it was my back yard. I can show you the best trails from now on.' He swung his horse, stopped it again as Chisholm sat where he was.

'Want to catch yore breath a minute first, eh? Quite a climb, all right, but we're right about at the top. Mighty fine view from here, if it wasn't rainin'.'

'Yeah,' Chisholm agreed, and where Silver had turned to the right, he swung his horse, off to the left. Now, after a momentary hesitation, Silver followed. His voice sounded puzzled.

'Pretty poor trail, that way,' he suggested. 'A lot better this way.'

'That's why I prefer the other,' Chisholm answered. 'Not so apt to run into a bullet marked Sunset.'

'I ain't seen hide nor hair of any of 'em,' Silver grunted. 'Doubt if they'd be out in a storm like this.'

'Lying won't get you anywhere with me, Silver,' Chisholm said, and the words brought Silver up short, his head jerking like a gopher's at a hawk's shadow, a startled look overspreading his face.

'Lyin'?' he gasped. 'What you mean? Don't you trust me, boss—one o' yore own crew?'

'No,' Chisholm told him with equal abruptness. 'You're drawing Sunset pay, Silver—and you're here to lead me to my death. If you'd happened to see me before I did you, you'd have likely shot me in the back.'

Silver's jaw sagged, a look almost of panic was in his eyes for a moment. He tried to speak, gulped, and was wordless.

'No need of lying any more, Silver. It won't make a bit of difference.'

Silver was convinced. But his astonishment was great.

'H-how—what makes you think—'

'Everything,' Chisholm said. 'That cayuse is branded Trigger, but it hasn't been in the barn or corrals since I've been there, and you wouldn't go out and catch up a fresh horse in this storm—not with plenty in the barn. And you're all muddy. You started out, and met up with your boss—pulling out from the ranch when nobody was looking, as a spy, to tell Gallister that I was heading this way. He doesn't aim to overlook many bets, does he? And somewhere you had a spill. A bad tumble, looks like. No telling what it did to your horse—and saddle. So they fixed you up with another cayuse, with Trigger branded on it.'

Silver offered no denial. He gulped again.

'Must have been a bad spill,' Chisholm went on, 'to make you change saddles.'

'B-but—' Silver was past all subterfuge now, 'a saddle's a saddle—how in blazes—'

'There's blood on that saddle,' Chisholm pointed out. 'The rain hasn't washed it all away yet. Some of the blood that Pinto Lacey spilled when he was in it.'

Panic crept into Silver's face now, echoed in

166

his words.

'I—I—it's true, boss.' He choked. 'You sure ain't one to fool easy, are you? But I—I had to do it.' His face twisted miserably for a moment. 'I didn't want to—honest to Betsey I didn't. But they told me I—I had to. If I didn't they—they'd take me like they did Rafe—and beat my face off—then drag me in a rope—'

His voice rose almost to a scream.

'I couldn't help it. I aimed to warn you—'

The look on Chisholm's face stopped him as abruptly as his voice had risen.

'I told you that lying wouldn't do any good, not with me,' Chisholm repeated wearily. 'I hate a double-crosser,' he added. 'A man who fights on one side, doing a dirty job for pay, is bad enough. Still, if he does it in the open, he's not too bad. But a man who takes pay from both sides, and betrays like Judas, for thirty pieces of silver—'

He was silent a moment, looking at the twisted countenance of the other. Then his voice grew thoughtful.

'Silver,' he added. 'That's how you got your name, somewhere, is it? Betraying somebody else for silver?'

Silver shivered but offered no confirmation or denial. He seemed to have gone all to pieces now. Chisholm shook his head disgustedly.

'I can't shoot you down in cold blood,' he said. 'You aren't worth doing murder for. So you might as well keep riding, I guess. Only, if you want to go on living—better get clear of this country. A long way out.'

Silver brightened visibly.

'You going to let me go?' he whined. 'I—I sure won't do nothin' to ever make you regret it—'

'I'll make sure of that,' Chisholm agreed. 'Your horse looks fresher than mine. So we'll trade.'

Now, for the first time, naked terror washed across Silver's face. Under its influence, his features seemed to disintegrate, to twist formlessly. His voice was a shrill whine.

'No—no—you wouldn't do that—'

He caught himself then, panting like a dog. Chisholm's face was granite.

'We're trading,' he said. 'Now.' Added, not quite so gruffly, 'You can head where you please—down that way. And the storm's thick.'

Silver hesitated, then, lacking the will to challenge the man before him, dismounted. He climbed into the buckskin's saddle like an old man, looked again at Chisholm, and wistfully back the way he had come. Chisholm relented a little.

'Go where you please,' he said.

With something like a sob, Silver did so, swinging toward the left. For a few moments he let his horse pick its way. Then all at once he was spurring, riding as though a host of devils was behind him.

The clatter of the horse's hoofs came back, on a rocky stretch of ground. Silver and the cayuse were almost out of sight, indistinct in the storm, when there came a rapid rattle of gunfire from the slash of the coulee. In the noise of it, Silver tried to shout, but his voice rose to a scream, was choked short off. And then, so far as Chisholm could see, the buckskin still ran on, but riderless now.

CHAPTER TWENTY-TWO

While the echoes still rolled and drummed, muted by the storm, Chisholm was riding, going as quietly as possible, down the slope as well, but heading in an opposite direction. Silver had started to lead him to where the others were ready and waiting, so that they could shoot him down. To play the same part as a Judas steer, even while protesting his good intentions.

It hadn't worked quite that way. He had tried at the last to dodge them, but some of them must have shifted around, and, seeing a man riding fast on a buckskin cayuse, they had reacted as Silver had expected. And the terror in him had caused him to make a wild run for it, rather than using caution.

Now it gave Chisholm a little respite. By the time the killers discovered their mistake, he should be past them, in the covering storm;

and, with a fresh horse under him, they'd have a hard time stopping him now. Confident that he was out of hearing, with soft sod underfoot and fairly level ground again, he put the black to a run.

There was a good chance now that those who had been after him were behind, with no one in front, but he did not relax his vigilance. After all, this merely postponed showdown.

Gallister would have his crew over here—with these same gunmen as a part of it—to get the Trigger herd and crowd them up the trail to the reservation. And now he would have been told the thing which Chisholm had hoped to keep a secret—that Chisholm planned to get help from Bill Gordy's 79.

But there was no help for it, and, if Gordy was the man that Sandra believed him to be, that wouldn't make any difference to him. Nor, Chisholm was sure, would the thing that Judge Wood had done make a difference, or even particularly surprise him. Bill Gordy was evidently basing his judgment of Sandra on what he knew of her personally. He would probably long since have guessed that any judge on the bench in Red Rock was there only because Sunset approved.

There was no diminishing of the storm as the day wore on, but in it Chisholm encountered no one. Now, though it was his ally as well, the rain was a hindrance, for it was difficult to see any landmarks, such as had been mentioned, by which to guide himself. A butte could be passed close at hand and be invisible, and lesser objects were like wraiths.

But with darkfall not far off, he knew that he was on a ranch again, and presently he caught the faint glow of a lamp in a window. These were log buildings—a big barn, a bunkhouse, two or three outbuildings, and, off a little way, a new log house, so new that it was still shiny.

'Must be a good grove of trees, off in here,' Chisholm reflected. 'And all of it fits, except this new house. Guess I can understand that, too. Must be Seventy-nine, all right.'

He dismounted, stiffly, by the bunkhouse, called out. Someone threw open the door.

'Light and come in, stranger,' was the hearty invitation. 'Here, we'll have somebody put yore cayuse in the barn.' He looked keenly from Chisholm to the horse. 'Trigger?' he asked.

'Yeah,' Chisholm agreed. 'Is this the Seventy-nine?'

'Sure is. Must be somethin' mighty pressin' to bring you out on a day like this.'

'I was hoping to find track of a herd of ours, over this way,' Chisholm explained.

'Sure, they're off near the canyon. My name's Fisher,' he added, as another man went out and led the horse away. 'I'm foreman, here.'

'Glad to know you, Fisher,' Chisholm agreed, shaking hands. 'I'm Chisholm—

171

foreman at Trigger. I hope Gordy's home?'

Some of the friendliness seemed to fall away from Fisher. He was a big, hearty man, with a hospitable way, but that last remark had not been too well received.

'Foreman?' he repeated. 'Yeah—Gordy's home. But I thought Pinto Lacey was foreman there—lately?'

'He was,' Chisholm agreed, 'but Trigger is run by Molly Benton again. Not by Sunset. And Lacey's dead.'

Fisher blinked, then his smile came back and he shook hands all over again.

'That so?' he exclaimed. 'That's the best news I've heard in a month o' Sundays. Come on across to the house. Gordy, he'll be mighty glad to hear that, too.'

Chisholm followed him across to the new house. Inside, a big stove glowed cheerfully, but the place was even more resplendent with newness, and there was little furniture, save in the kitchen, where a few old pieces had been brought in. Gordy himself, a tall, black-haired man, was making faces at himself in a small mirror, shaving. He turned, one side of his face still covered with lather, as the door opened.

'Bill,' Fisher said familiarly, 'this is Chisholm, from Trigger. He says he's foreman there now, and that Pinto Lacey's dead. Likewise, that Sunset ain't runnin' Trigger any longer—that Molly Benton has taken over again.'

Gordy stared for a moment, at this news. Then a smile creased his own face, and he held out his hand, transferring his razor to the other.

'That so? Mighty glad to hear it, Chisholm— mighty glad. And glad to know you.' His eyes narrowed. 'You ride all the way here today, in this storm? Rustle him up some clothes, Pat. Get those off, here by the fire. Pat'll have some dry ones, time you're out of 'em.'

So Chisholm changed, while Gordy finished shaving. He gave him a brief account of the change at Trigger, since none of that news had reached this far, then went on to explain something of the coming of the railroad, and on to the beef herd which was to be sold to the government for the Indians on the reservation.

'Sounds just like Gallister,' Gordy nodded. 'And you aim to stop him with the herd, I suppose? But where's your crew, man? Are they outside?'

'They're home,' Chisholm said. 'I came alone. They have to guard Trigger.'

Bill Gordy fingered his newly shaven chin thoughtfully.

'Guess you're right,' he agreed. 'But— alone? What on earth—'

'I'd better tell you a little more about myself,' Chisholm added, and did so. Gordy snorted with indignation at the tale of how he had been sentenced to hang, then sobered.

'You say Judge Wood did that?' he asked.

'Yeah.' Chisholm chose his words carefully. 'Then he got drunk—good and drunk. I figure he didn't like it, but that Gallister had him whipsawed.'

'Likely,' Gordy nodded, then grinned. 'Don't look like they hung you, at that.'

'No.' Chisholm went on with the explanation, to where it involved Sandra.

'That took the most courage of anything that I ever saw anybody do,' he added. 'To say what she did, to us there this morning. But she told it. Said you'd wanted her to set you a task, like fair ladies did their knights of old—something hard to do. Looked to me like she loved you—and I've a hunch that you've built this house, new, for her—and to kind of surprise her?'

Gordy colored, then nodded.

'Yeah—that's what I've been hopin' for,' he conceded. 'Aim to let her pick out the furniture and fixin's she wants. But you say—what was that again?'

'She thought you and your men would help me at this end of the line.' Chisholm allowed that to sink in for a moment, went on. 'It hit her hard—awfully hard, about her father. She idolized him. Finding that he had feet of clay—it wasn't easy. Now she's not sure that you'd want to have anything to do with any member of her family, after a thing like that had happened.'

'Blazes!' Gordy said explosively. 'I'm

174

marryin' her, if she'll have me—not her dad. And I knew all along that he had to do what Gallister told him, to hold his job.'

'I thought you'd figure that way. But in her present state of mind, she wants a test—to be real sure, sure that you do care for her, anyhow. And then too, as I see it, she is turning to you, as the man she loves, to help her extirpate the guilt that she feels.'

Bill Gordy was silent a long moment, considering that angle of it. Then he grinned.

'Blazes!' he repeated. 'The boys'll think it's a picnic—special if Sunset puts up a scrap! And I'll like nothing better than a good excuse to tangle with Gallister!' From the light in his eyes, Chisholm knew that this was an old score.

'But you must be starved,' he added. 'Supper ought to be about ready. We'll go over and eat with the boys and tell 'em about it.'

They did so, and the response was all that Chisholm had been led to expect. He had never seen a finer looking bunch of cowboys, or men that he liked better on first sight. There were five of them, not including Fisher or the cook, and the prospect of excitement was like tempting kids with candy. Though it was likely that Sunset's gun crew would outnumber them two to one, that prospect did not seem to daunt them for a moment.

'We'll get right down there to the canyon and start roundin' the herd up, come mornin',' Fisher declared, thumping the table till the dishes jumped. 'And if they want a fight—let 'em try it!'

The others whooped and echoed the sentiment. Chisholm looked at them soberly.

'Likely to be heavy odds,' he pointed out.

'But you don't seem to be stoppin' on that account.' Fisher grinned.

'It's a little different with me. I'm in this up to my neck. It's my job.'

'It's going to be our job, too,' Gordy assured him. 'All the way to the reservation.'

'Thanks. But I've been thinking—Gallister's pretty sure to have his men on the job in the morning, starting the roundup, which is quite a chore.'

'Yeah. But I don't reckon we can divide that,' Fisher said dryly. 'I wouldn't want their help, and I doubt if they'd cotton to us.'

'That isn't what I meant. The weather'll be bad for another day, maybe two. Rounding the herd up and getting them started is going to be particularly mean in the storm. But Sunset'll have the crew to do it. So why not let them? We'll keep out of sight—which is apt to make them jittery—keep ourselves warm and dry, and let 'em do it. And they can do most of the driving to the reservation, too. After all, that's where we want the cattle delivered.'

The others were watching him expectantly now. The shadow of a grin creased Bill Gordy's face.

'And then?' he breathed.

'Then, when the right time comes—we'll spook the herd into a stampede,' Chisholm suggested. 'Let 'em run—toward the reservation. Only, from there on out, we'll take them in!'

CHAPTER TWENTY-THREE

The others had approved with loud-voiced enthusiasm. They had been perfectly willing to fight it out in the morning, to go through all the disagreeable work of rounding up the big herd in the storm and making the drive. But the notion of allowing their rivals to do most of the dirty work, while the storm was at its peak, and then profiting by it at their leisure, appealed to them hugely.

By the next morning, the storm still showed no signs of abating. A couple of the cowboys rode out in it, to return later with the report that Sunset was very busy with the roundup—at least a score of them at work, under difficulties.

For, as Chisholm was well aware, working cattle in such a storm was about as mean a job as could be found. The weather made tempers short for men and horses and cows alike, and slipping and sliding at every turn, with the rain soaking them, made it that much worse. But a time limit had been set for delivery of the herd, and that date would not wait on the weather.

Likewise, the knowledge that Chisholm would act, if they did not, would spur them on.

'They didn't see ary sign of us,' one of the scouts reported. 'We took good care of that. But they're sure watchful as a dog with a fresh bone. Spend a lot of time lookin' for trouble that ain't there—yet!'

The interlude gave Chisholm a chance to stay indoors and rest. By the following day, the rain had stopped, though the skies were still gray and lowering, the air remained damp and raw, and the mud was thick underfoot— weather in which cattle would stay boogery, hard to drive. But the Sunset crew, whatever their shortcomings, could do the work they were hired for. The big herd had been gathered and held, and now they were starting the final drive toward the reservation.

With Bill Gordy as guide, Chisholm took a look, from a vantage point where they could see but not be easily seen. One thing was plain. The complete absence of any interference, up to now, had not reassured Symes Gallister. His whole outfit was raw with tension, momentarily expecting anything to happen.

'And when men feel that way, the critters get the feelin' mighty quick too.' Fisher nodded wisely. 'They'll all be ready to jump and run if you so much as say scat!'

'We'll give them another day,' Chisholm decided. 'This is a lot easier job than I'd counted on, up to now.'

The sun came out briefly that afternoon, then was gone again like a will-o'-the-wisp. The next morning it shone brightly, with warm promise, but within half an hour haze was beginning to obscure it. There was the feel of more storm in the air, of unfinished business by the rain makers. By afternoon, it was cloudy again, with a fitful wind ruffling the grass, moaning eerily in the treetops. Leaves shook with a soft leathery rustle which told of fall and had the promise of winter inherent in it. And the big herd, despite nearly three days of herding, showed no signs of settling down to steady plodding.

'We'll let them camp, then wait till near morning,' Chisholm told the eager crew who clustered behind him. 'Then, just before daylight, we'll jump them.'

Gordy shot a look at him.

'You claim to be a lawyer,' he said dryly, 'but you sure seem to know cattle, and this sort of business.'

'Guess I haven't forgotten all I once knew,' Chisholm conceded, and turned to his host. 'I certainly appreciate what you're doing. And I know how busy you are right now, too. Taking time off to help us out is something we won't forget.'

'We can always work, soon as the herd's delivered,' Gordy said. 'As for the rest, there's such a thing as bein' neighborly. And I figure I'm doing this as much for myself as for you, anyhow.' He grinned. 'Here you had me all het up. Big, difficult job—but heck! The way you're handlin' it, they'll have themselves all wore out 'fore we get to them. Won't be nothin' to it.'

There was something to that, and Chisholm was counting on it. The need for constant vigilance, of a big crew to ride night herd and be on guard as well, was wearing Gallister's men down. They were all close to exhaustion, short of sleep, frayed of nerves. Chisholm and the 79, on the other hand, were fresh and eager to go.

Night closed down early, drawing in from all sides and above like a great blanket. The threat of fresh storm was in the air, but so far nothing had happened. Here the nature of the land was changing, as they neared the reservation, now about ten miles away. This was canyonlike country. What had been a wide valley, with occasional clumps of cottonwoods or now and then a sentinel pine, had drawn together so that it was never more than a quarter of a mile wide, frequently less. The encompassing hills were higher, steeper. There was a creek, fed by smaller tributaries, though the water, even here, was brackish and poor in quality, like that at Red Rock.

From the crest of the canyon, himself out of sight, Chisholm observed the camp below. The riders were trying to soothe the herd, circling it, singing in hoarse, cracked voices. But, tired as

180

men and cattle alike were, the tension had continued to build up until now it was near the breaking point. Voices, clear in the unnaturally still air, floated up to Chisholm.

'If anything's going to happen, it'll have to be pretty soon.' That was Gallister, his voice tight and brittle.

'Yeah. Reckon likely.' Tate Dunning sounded calm and undisturbed. 'Rain before morning.'

'Damn the rain!' Gallister swore. 'If he's going to do anything, I wish he'd get at it! And listen to those fools! How can they expect to quiet cattle with their voices like files? It'd scare a jackass to death.'

'Yeah,' Dunning agreed. 'Think you could do any better?'

For answer, Gallister swore at him, and, in the dimly reflected light of a fire, they saw him move away. Pat Fisher, beside Chisholm, chuckled.

'Just about ripe for the pickin',' he said.

'Let's get some sleep,' Chisholm yawned. 'They're missing enough for both of us.'

An hour before dawn they were aprowl, drinking strong, hot coffee, eating a hasty breakfast. Not until the horses were saddled and they were gathered around him did Chisholm give final orders.

'Pat and I will stampede the herd,' he said. 'The rest of you be on down ahead a mile or so, to gather them up and keep 'em moving. If

181

we're lucky—fine. But you'll know what to do when the time comes, well as I could say. So I guess that's it.'

'Give us twenty minutes.' Gordy nodded, peered laconically at the dark pile of clouds overhead as he swung his horse. 'Looks like luck's ridin' with us,' he added. 'Something's going to bust loose, right soon!'

They waited, while the hoofbeats of the crew receded, were swallowed in the gloom. This was the hour when daylight should be crowding the east, breaking the shackles of the night. Instead, the faint grayness that had been apparent when they breakfasted was lost now in an even thicker pall. Somewhere, despite the lateness of the season, thunder growled.

'Let's move,' said Chisholm. He could barely see his companion beside him as they rode. Ahead, presently, they could hear a vague, uneasy stir—the herd. The cattle sensed the coming storm and were fearful of it. And, from the sound, it was apparent that the full crew of Sunset was not yet awake to help. Suddenly, with a few preliminary drops of rain, the storm hit.

It came in a wild burst of driving rain, which seemed to be shaken loose by a gigantic clap of thunder. The whole earth shook with it, and lightning poured like liquid lava from a caldron poised above the earth, seeming to spray down at them in a wild magnificence. It revealed the herd, eyes glaring redly, on their

182

feet and ready for trouble. And then, as more lightning was uncorked at them, the two men hit the edge of the herd, shouting, shooting off their guns.

Gordy had brought along a stick of dynamite, with the notion that it might be useful. But Chisholm had been pretty certain that it would not be needed this time, and he was right. It took only their yelling, on top of the wild flaring lightning, the still shaking thunder, to do the trick. Snorting, bawling in frenzy, the cattle nearest to them turned, hurtled pell-mell into the middle of the milling mass, and then, so quickly that it seemed incredible, the whole herd was in wild motion, complete stampede, and going the way Chisholm wanted them to go.

Now the confusion was indescribable. There was nothing that anybody could do, but Chisholm spurred hard on the heels of the fleeing cattle, knowing that Fisher would do the same. The rain was a solid sheet of water, and in it the whole camp behind them was in a state of panic. It would take some time before they could sort themselves out, saddle horses and even try to pursue.

Within a mile, the worst of the rain was past, though lightning still made a wild display. But the storm was already moving off, away from them. And now the daylight, held back, broke triumphantly through the cloud wrack and showed the herd, still closely bunched, hurtling

183

along like a wild juggernaut.

Shadowy figures were closing in on either side, though the canyon itself did most of it—silent men who rode watchfully with them, taking care only to keep the cattle bunched and headed in the right direction.

There was not a single Sunset cowboy with the herd now, or around to challenge their taking over the herd. That part had been accomplished without the firing of a shot, except for the first banging of guns to help start the stampede.

CHAPTER TWENTY-FOUR

Bill Gordy swung his horse alongside, elation in his face, though he was careful to keep his voice down. It was all right to let the cattle run, so long as they felt like it, but not to add to their excitement.

'I never saw a thing go off smoother!' he chortled. 'Sure caught them flat-footed!'

It was true, and Chisholm was well pleased. But it was too soon to crow. Sunset had been fooled, though, with the building storm to booger the cattle, it had been something which no crew, however skilled and alert, could have done much against. But they would soon be coming, and more than ever ready to fight.

Only a few drops of rain spattered out of suddenly empty skies now. Blue was overhead, as though a dark blanket had been torn wide open. Sunshine poured through. The hoarse bawling of the cattle, as they ran, was dwindling, their pace was slowing. Some four miles had already been covered, and they would run another two or three, at dwindling speed, before slowing to a walk again. But their panic was past.

Looking back, down the canyon, Chisholm could see Sunset, in the saddle at last and coming. But they were only riding at a steady trot, determined and purposeful. A few minutes one way or the other did not mean much now.

Unless—and sudden hope rose in Chisholm. Maybe this was one factor that even Gallister had overlooked. By the time they caught up, everyone would be in full sight of the reservation. There would be the Indian agent there, and McQuade as well. Men with official standing. As well as several hundred Indians, all watching the arrival of the big herd with lively anticipation.

Before such an audience, even Gallister would hardly dare to open a gun-battle. For if it came now, he would have to start it.

The same thought had come to Gallister. He turned, scowling, to where the cheerfully imperturbable Tate Dunning rode beside him. Dunning had found time to shave, some time the previous evening. He looked as fresh and untroubled as though there had been no four or five hectic days on the trail, in comparison to the reddened eyes, the rough whiskers and generally disheveled appearance of all the rest of the crew—including Gallister. And that fact did nothing to improve his employer's temper.

'You act like you was tickled about it all!' he snarled. 'And what are we going to do? I'd figured on shooting it out, if they got up nerve to attack. Now we can't even do that!'

'Nope, wouldn't look right,' Dunning agreed.

'Well, what the devil are we going to do?' Gallister demanded angrily. 'Let him get away with it?'

'Nothin' to get excited about, is there? More than one way of skinnin' a cat, I've always heard.'

Gallister eyed him for a moment. Then the echo of Dunning's sardonic grin showed briefly in his own eyes.

'Guess you're right, at that, Tate,' he agreed.

Chisholm could tell, soon after, that they had decided on new strategy. He was relieved, particularly on account of Bill Gordy and his crew. The one thing that had really worried him was the prospect of an armed clash between them and Sunset gunnies. That 79 would give a good account of themselves in such a battle, he had no doubt. But in the last analysis, it wasn't their fight. Now that clash, he was pretty sure, would be averted. But when Gallister resorted to indirect methods, he was

186

always most dangerous.

Now the herd was slowing, tired from the long strain of the last few days, their excitement all run out in the last hour, and anxious to stop and eat, or to sink down and rest. But they would keep going without much trouble to their destination, now so close at hand.

Behind, but still closing the gap, came Sunset. Now the Indians, many of them mounted on their own wiry little cayuses, were starting out to meet the herd, to take over. That insured that there would be no open clash of arms. But Gallister came on as steadily as though nothing untoward had happened.

'Me, I'm sort of disappointed,' Fisher confided. 'Here I'd looked for some fun out of this—but it's been pretty tame.'

'Maybe it's not over,' Gordy cautioned.

'There comes McQuade,' Fisher said. 'Journey's end.'

Sunset was closing up with them now. If McQuade was surprised at the sight of the two rival claimants, he gave no sign of it. He had spent the night snugly in the agent's headquarters, and he was shaven and comfortable. His big new Stetson was carefully fitted to hide the baldness of his head, the inevitable cigar cocked at an angle in his mouth. His eyes raked the herd with cool expertness.

'Tryin' to run the fat all off 'em?' was his

greeting.

'They broke away and stampeded when that storm hit, this morning,' Chisholm explained, and found Gallister almost beside him. Gallister made no attempt to deny that, however, and McQuade gave him a short, curt nod of greeting. The two crews were eying each other warily, but that was all.

'At least, they're here,' McQuade observed. 'We'll make a count, and pay.'

With the Indians to help, it was easy to handle the herd as they pleased now. With McQuade himself, the reservation agent, Chisholm, Bill Gordy, Gallister and Tate Dunning all checking, the count was made. Approximately a thousand head, as contracted for. There was a difference of only two head between the figures which any of them reported.

'Close enough,' McQuade agreed. 'I'm not one to haggle over a difference like that.' He eyed them sharply. 'Who's supposed to be sellin' this herd?'

'You bought 'em of me, as I recollect,' Gallister said.

'But I delivered them—and have a bill of sale from the owner, properly made out,' Chisholm interposed, and passed it over to McQuade.

'That's no good,' Gallister observed shortly.

'Good enough for me,' McQuade decided. 'I agreed to pay the money to the man who delivered the cattle. Chisholm has them, and a legal bill of sale.'

'Well, I suppose I can't stop you, if that's the way you feel about it,' Gallister shrugged. 'But I must make formal protest, and claim to the money.'

'I told you the same thing,' McQuade reminded him. 'That I'd pay the money to whoever delivered the herd. You agreed to that. Come on with me to the agency, Mr Chisholm, and it will be ready.'

Gallister shrugged, swung his horse and rode away, followed by his men. Bill Gordy looked after them uneasily.

'I don't like the looks of that,' he said. 'Don't like it at all. He's takin' it too easy.'

'Maybe I'm speakin' out of turn—but wouldn't it be a good idea for Mr McQuade to hold the money here, till some other time when you want to pick it up?' Fisher interposed.

McQuade's lips tightened.

'I'm paying the money now, and taking your receipt,' he said. 'I don't propose to be involved in this any farther. I've kept my agreement, as I told both of you I would handle it, and as you both agreed to. If you don't want the money, then I'll pay it to Gallister.'

'I'll take it,' Chisholm agreed. 'It's what I came for.'

Inside the agency, he received the money, a fair-sized bundle in bills of large denomination, and wrote out a receipt for it. Then he carefully tucked the money inside his

189

coat, and followed Gordy out into the open again.

'Well, that's that—so far,' Gordy said soberly. 'They did all the hard work, and you get the money. Which has made 'em plenty sore. They'll try and take it away from you before you get home, sure as fate. So I guess it's up to us to ride along with you. I was wantin' a good excuse for comin' up that way and seein' Sandra again, anyhow.'

Chisholm smiled, but shook his head.

'Thanks, Bill,' he said. 'But you've done all I asked, all I wanted. And I know you've let your own work go to do it. I'll manage now.'

'But—blazes, man,' Gordy protested. 'You know they ain't quittin' yet.'

'I know. And if it comes to trouble—you boys would put up a good fight for me. I appreciate that. But in that case, it would be an open gun-battle, to the last man. And when they came, they would outnumber us three to one. We couldn't dodge it, a big crew. And we couldn't win it.'

'We could do a good job tryin',' Gordy said. 'What chance have you got, alone, if all of us couldn't make it through?'

'The chance of dodging them,' Chisholm pointed out. 'One man alone can move pretty quiet. Six or seven couldn't miss being caught. So I'll do it that way. I'll ride with you till night camp, then pull on out when it gets dark. It'll be around fifty miles, straight across country.

By noon tomorrow, with luck, I'll be at Trigger.'

'And if you don't get there, I'll hunt Gallister down and kill him, if it's the last thing I do,' Gordy swore. 'Though that won't help you none then.'

Nor would it help the warm-hearted Gordy, if it ever came to that, Chisholm knew. He'd do his best, in such a contest. But Symes Gallister, head of a crew of gunhawks, maintained that position because he was the toughest man of them all. In a straight shoot-out, Bill Gordy would stand no chance at all.

CHAPTER TWENTY-FIVE

As Chisholm had counted on, Sunset had kept out of sight for the remainder of that day. It was a long way back to Trigger, and what they had to do Gallister would prefer to try well away from where any witnesses might be handy.

Again, over supper, Bill Gordy made an attempt to dissuade him, and when he had failed, announced his intention of at least seeing that Chisholm got a good start.

'Chances are, there's one or more of them sidewinders spyin' on us right now, figgerin' you'll try pullin' out in the dark,' he said. 'So we'll all ride off, in as many diff'rent directions, when you start. And they'll earn their money if they pick you out and hold to yore trail!'

That was a real service, and Chisholm appreciated it. If he could be sure of getting a good start, without being trailed, then he'd stand a reasonably good chance. But he knew too much of Gallister to believe for a moment that the battle would be won so easily. Gallister would have sent word ahead to Sunset, for others of his picked gunmen to be out and on the watch. And with his own riders, he would be somewhere in the country between, all of them keeping a sharp watch for Chisholm when he came along.

That would be playing fox and hounds for the highest stake. Not only the money in his pocket, but his life as well. Every setback which Sunset suffered only brought the inevitable showdown that much closer. And by now, things had built up to the point where it had to be settled in blood.

At a little before midnight, when the darkness was heavy, they pulled out, moving as silently as possible, each horse and rider heading off in a different direction. The 79 crew would keep going, gradually swinging to meet again a few miles farther on and camp for the rest of the night.

Before he had ridden far, Chisholm was certain that the ruse had worked. Any watchers had been baffled, and he was well away. For the remainder of the night, unless he blundered into one of the watchers, he would be reasonably secure.

There were high thin clouds, broken at times, but it was warmer, and the ground, still well soaked but no longer soggy, was like a sponge under the hoofs of his horse, as nearly soundless as he could hope for. Chisholm rode steadily, alertly. Gallister wanted that money. It meant a lot, and the personal score between the two of them was even higher, though defeat in this one matter would not mean overmuch to Sunset. Gallister still held strong trump cards, and he was playing chiefly for Trigger itself and the juicy plum of the railroad. Even if Chisholm got there safely, the big settlement would still remain.

It was well past midnight when his horse pricked up its ears, and Chisholm was quick to note the sign. He had heard nothing, for his own part, but this was a likely place for trouble. Here was an easy pass through some hills, and apparently one or more watchers had been set to guard the pass.

To swing and circle, climbing, seemed the sensible thing. And then there came the sudden sharp crack of a gun, and he knew that he had been seen.

The gunman's aim had been hasty, for Chisholm did not even hear the bullet pass him. But as he turned and gave his horse its head, he could tell from the sounds that at least three or four riders were on his trail now, not far behind. Another minute, and he would have ridden into a trap.

To escape them might not be easy. They had the advantage both of numbers and of knowing the country, as well as fresher horses. Another bullet came close enough so that he could hear its eerie whistle in passing, then the shooting subsided. Behind, he could make them out as only a faint blur, and to their eyes he would be less than that.

And then he had a piece of luck. He saw them, off at the side, and for an instant he had a sinking feeling that now he was trapped, that here were more horsemen waiting, where they could pounce down on him. Then he saw that these were cattle, not horses—perhaps a score of them. Probably they had been bedded down for the night, but the shooting and the sound of running horses had roused them. Now they were standing up, undecided, but ready to run.

A moment later Chisholm burst in among them, setting them to running. He kept with them, silent, bending low, indistinguishable from the others at a little distance. It was not long until the inevitable happened. A small bunch to begin with, and with plenty of room, they started to spread out, heading in different directions. It was the same trick as earlier in the night, with a new variation.

Presently he knew that it had worked again. His pursuers were somewhere behind, hopelessly confused. And now it was unlikely that any more would be in front of him, between him and Trigger. He must have come through the line of watchers. It was that which decided him to keep going. By steady pushing, he could reach Trigger by morning. Stopping to sleep for a while would be just as risky. Better to get it over with.

The passing miles seemed to vindicate his judgment. He paused a couple of times, to loosen the cinch and allow his horse to crop a brief lunch, and he ate a little from the supplies which he carried. Day came, with bright sunshine, revealing a country which seemed to be made up of far spaces. Not far now to Trigger.

His impulse was to spur, and it was hard to restrain. He was, he discovered, and somewhat to his own amazement, hugely impatient to reach Trigger—more so than he had been to get anywhere, or to see anyone, in a long time. And he admitted the reason to himself. It was because Molly Benton would be there.

Through the years he had trained himself to steady, practical thoughts. Now, for a little while, he relaxed, allowed the luxury of daydreams to course through his head. For now, for the first time, he had something to dream about.

He brought up with a jerk, conscious that he had allowed his guard to drop, thinking too much of other things. This was Trigger—he knew the land, but it was still a few miles on to the ranch buildings. And from out of a coulee a horseman had suddenly ridden to confront him. Brick Hogarth.

Hogarth lounged in the saddle now, confident and easy. There was the same good-natured light in his eyes, the same pleasant smile on his face that had been there when Chisholm had talked to him in the town jail. He looked boyish and a little shy, anything but what he was—a killer with many notches on his gun. And Chisholm knew, without being told, what Hogarth was here for. To kill him.

The confidence of the man was superb. He could have shot from ambush, dropping Chisholm before he suspected that there was anyone around. But Brick Hogarth did not consider anything like that as being necessary. And, in his way, he had a code of his own. Now he nodded cheerfully.

'Sort of figured you'd give 'em the slip and get this far, Chisholm,' he said. 'You're a lot smarter than most folks give you credit for.'

'Think so?' Chisholm asked, warily. 'I'm sorry to see you here, Brick.'

'Kind of sorry, myself,' Hogarth conceded. 'You did me a good turn once—or anyway, you thought you did. I've kept hopin' that it wouldn't come to this.'

'You could still ride away, if you liked. I wouldn't stop you.'

That, as he had expected, seemed to amuse Hogarth hugely. He grinned broadly, then sobered.

'No, I don't reckon you'd stop me,' he said. 'But I was told to stop you. And when you take wages for doing a job, you do it. That's the way I look at it.'

It was, and Chisholm gave him credit for it, a job which he would have preferred not to do. But that would not make him hesitate an instant when it came to squeezing trigger. This was merely a part of the day's work. He would shoot a coyote or a man, either one, with the same skill, the same lack of emotion. In this case, he had felt a sense of obligation, and that had induced him to offer this explanation. That was the only difference.

'You didn't quite understand, Brick,' Chisholm said, his tone sharpening. 'Are you so sure that I couldn't stop you—or that I can't?'

Hogarth looked astonished, then amused.

'You're a pretty good lawyer, Chisholm,' he said. 'But when it comes to guns—they're my business.'

Chisholm considered him for a long moment. It had been over Hogarth that he had been first tricked, made a fool of. He had helped get the gunman free, after a completely cold-blooded killing. Yet he would have gone free in any case. He richly deserved the fate that he had dealt out to others, but regret was in Chisholm. Aside from the utterly emotionless 'business' that Hogarth was in, he was a

197

pleasant fellow always.

'Maybe guns are my business, too.' Chisholm nodded. 'I took up the law to get away from them—they seemed so senseless. But did you ever hear of the Dakota Kid, Brick?'

Slowly, Brick's eyes widened.

'You mean—the fastest gunman the Dakotas ever knew?' he breathed. 'You—' incredulity was in his voice. 'You ain't him?'

Chisholm nodded.

'That's what they used to call me.'

He had held hopes, but thin ones. Now they stretched taut and broke as the smile widened Hogarth's face again.

'Well, call me a mossyhorn!' he chuckled. 'Downin' the Dakota Kid will be somethin' for even me to brag about!'

CHAPTER TWENTY-SIX

There was no choice now. Hogarth was supremely confident of himself. And any faint compunctions which he had felt toward a lawyer who had tried to help him were gone now in this new revelation. His face went taut and harsh.

'Let's see some of that famous speed, Kid,' he said. 'You'll need it!'

His draw was something to wonder at, a thing of blinding speed even while Hogarth

198

twisted half around and threw himself to one side, all in a concerted motion. But there had been others, and Chisholm had lost none of the skill which had so sickened him of the whole business in the past. Only one gun spoke.

He saw, with more of regret than exultation, the way in which Hogarth's spin was checked. The speed and sureness seemed to go out of him, leaving him for a moment like a man become suddenly tired and hesitant. For a slow heartbeat, his hand held on to the gun which had cleared leather, and his face twisted with the effort of will to raise it the necessary few inches. Fury, and something of hurt surprise, blended across his face. Then his fingers unclasped, his knees buckled, and it was over.

Smoke was curling up like a welcoming beacon as Chisholm came in sight of the buildings. He was met by Rafe and Andy, riding out pell-mell, full of eager questions.

'Knew you'd make it, and hawg all the fun,' Rafe declared. 'Ain't been a thing goin' on here to break the monotony. 'Cept that Silver's missin', and them two from the railroad was here to see you ag'in yesterday.'

'They seemed right anxious to see you, too,' Andy added. 'Said they'd be back ag'in today.'

Then he saw Molly, standing out on the porch, and this other news seemed flat by comparison. She had no greeting for him as he came up—only stood there and looked at him, and there was something in her eyes which was

199

far deeper than words. A sort of wistful hunger, a soft thanksgiving shining there, as though she had hoped but had scarcely dared expect that he would return.

There was much to talk about, but not much time for it. Nellie brought breakfast, a bountiful meal, and he was in the middle of that when she came back in to announce that 'them railroaders is here again.'

John Thomas was sartorial perfection today, even to the part in his glossy whiskers. Superintendent Lang seemed less concerned with his personal appearance than his comfort. He shook hands, acknowledged introductions, then, with a sigh, sank into a chair.

'Coffee!' he said. 'With the aroma of nectar! If I could have a cup of that, I'd be a new man again!'

'There's plenty of it.' Nellie beamed, serving both of them. 'And how about a stack of hot cakes, along with Mr Chisholm? Wouldn't go bad, after drivin' way out here, would they?'

'I would feel like two new men, then,' Lang declared, and Nellie scurried to fetch the cakes. In the kitchen again, she turned to Rafe.

'If you'd just learn to talk pretty like that,' she pointed out, 'a woman could take pride in havin' you around. Sayin' he'd feel like two new men, with some good breakfast. My land, ain't that poetic?'

'Looks like two men, too,' Rafe grumbled. 'Way he bulges over that chair, I was lookin' for it to bust. Likely do it, yet.'

Little was said until breakfast was out of the way. Lang ate thoughtfully, contentedly. Thomas talked lightly of this and that. But Chisholm could tell that something was on their minds. With the meal ended, Thomas wiped his whiskers carefully and revealed it.

'We've been very anxious to see you, Mr Chisholm,' he declared. 'Careful investigation has convinced us that what you told us the other day is correct. But, as a lawyer, you are perfectly well aware that justice is not always done.'

'That happens far too often,' Chisholm conceded.

'Exactly. We would prefer to deal with you and Miss Benton—or Mrs Gallister. But something has come up—it isn't necessary to go into details, except to say that it concerns our franchise from the government, with a time limit which we had been led to expect would be much more liberal. Now, quite frankly, we are going to be pinched for time. And because of that, various of our stockholders, influential men, and well-meaning—but with very little practical knowledge of this country or the conditions which we face—they are presenting difficulties—and ultimatums!'

'In other words,' Lang added quietly, 'we can't wait. We've got to get title to a right of way across Trigger, to be assured that there will be no slip-up. Otherwise, the directors insist on an alternate route, running more than a hundred miles to the south. It isn't nearly so good, but there are no legal difficulties involved. We have to have title, from either you or Gallister, not later than tomorrow.'

'And it has to be a clear, foolproof affair, which the other party cannot attack,' Thomas added. 'We have sent word to Mr Gallister to the same effect. Unless this can be settled, definitely and finally, we have no choice in the matter.'

Chisholm could understand that. Eastern stockholders, understanding nothing of the difficulties, interested only in profits, could be very demanding at times. And, as Thomas said, when they presented an ultimatum, that left no choice.

'I'll go right in to town and see Judge Wood, today,' Chisholm promised. 'I think we can find a way to settle this to your entire satisfaction, gentlemen.'

'I sincerely hope so,' Thomas agreed. 'It would break my heart to have to give up this proposed route, which Mr Lang and I consider so much superior to the alternate southern route. But I'm afraid you face serious difficulties. Judge Wood is, er—rather difficult to see, these days.'

'He's a virtual prisoner in his own house,' Lang said bluntly, 'with a whole crew of Gallister's gun-hands keeping him so.'

'Gallister intends to force us to deal with

202

him, on his own terms,' Thomas added. 'He's somehow gotten wind of this time limit—and there you have it. If you can do anything— well, all I can say is that you'll be going some.'

Chisholm agreed with them. Here was a situation where Gallister stood to retrieve all his losses, and he was playing it for all that it was worth, with the judge virtually a prisoner. That might mean that Wood was inclined to protest, but he was being given no chance to do so. Chisholm looked up as Sandra entered the room, her face grave.

'That seems to be the size of it,' she agreed. 'I—I got to thinking things over, and decided that I had been too hard on Dad—running out on him without even giving him a chance to tell me his side of it. So yesterday afternoon I rode in to town to see him. And they wouldn't let me!'

'Then, if you'll excuse me, gentlemen—the sooner I get there, the better!' Chisholm said decisively. 'Rafe,' he called, 'if you figure you've been cheated before, you might come along now!'

'Be right with you,' Rafe agreed with alacrity. 'Sure need the exercise, anyhow.'

'How about the rest of us?' Andy asked anxiously. 'Sounds to me like it was a job for everybody.'

'Your job is to stay right here,' Chisholm cautioned. 'We have to hang on to Trigger till this is settled. Don't slip up on that.'

Nellie looked anxiously at Rafe, as he buckled on an extra gun.

'Mebby I was a mite mean, in some of them remarks, Rafe,' she said. 'I'm sorter gettin' used to havin' you under foot. Dunno but what I'd miss you if you wasn't here.'

'I aim to be,' Rafe assured her, and, boldly impulsive, leaned to kiss her furtively behind the ear. Outside, Molly looked at Chisholm.

'I don't like it,' she said. 'You've done too much for me already. I feel that I ought to go along, with this.'

'I'd rather have you here to come back to,' Chisholm said, and Molly, looking deep into his eyes, nodded.

'See that you come back to me,' she said, and it was a promise in itself. Turning suddenly, she went back into the house.

CHAPTER TWENTY-SEVEN

Red Rock looked peaceful, under the easy benediction of the sun. It was still an hour short of noon, and few people were in town at this time of day. But as they jogged past the judge's house, there was sudden stir to alertness of men lounging around it. No question but what Gallister's guards were there, and on the watch.

Without pausing, Chisholm rode past, then swung around the block. Rafe looked at him questioningly.

'Do we blast a way in?' he asked.

'If we have to,' Chisholm agreed. 'But we'll try something else first.' The county jail was before them, looking as unlovely as ever. But he dismounted, pushed to the door of the sheriff's office and flung it open. Sheriff Forbes, looking startled, stood up uncertainly from behind his desk.

'Are you going with us to see Judge Wood,' Chisholm asked quietly, 'or not?'

For a moment, sheer amazement held the sheriff silent. It was plain enough that he knew and understood the situation, that now he was torn between two possible courses. He opened his mouth, closed it again, and Chisholm saw a crafty light flicker in the back of his eyes for a moment. Then he nodded.

'Why, sure,' he agreed. 'No reason why not, I guess.'

Rafe eyed him with scant favor, but together, in silence, the three of them walked down the street to the judge's house again. A couple of guards were in front of the door, barring their way, and they eyed Forbes uncertainly. He nodded shortly.

'It's all right, boys,' he said. 'We're goin' in!'

They stood aside, and now Chisholm had the feeling that this was a door which would open only the one way—save for those who might come out, feet first. He saw the stealthy movement of a third figure, toward his gun,

205

and in that moment, Chisholm's own gun was out and at the base of the sheriff's neck.

'If anything happens, Sheriff,' he said cheerfully. 'It'll be to you first! Don't make any mistake about that.'

Forbes' florid face went chalky. For an instant he stood rigid, and from the corner of the house a skulking dog snarled, as the rank odor of fear came to its nostrils. Chisholm could sense the quaking fear in the man who had tried to lead them into a trap and had overlooked this possibility.

Then, stumbling a little, Forbes went on in, Chisholm and Rafe at his heels. It was impossible to close the door behind them, for the gunmen were crowding there now as well— like a pack of hounds ready to rend and tear, hesitant but doubly savage because of the check.

They stopped, and now the door was closing, penning them in. Chisholm's left hand was on the sheriff's left arm, holding him, the muzzle of his gun a clammily cold thing on the sheriff's neck. And in that silence, curtains across an open doorway parted, and Judge Wood stood there, blinking a little uncertainly.

It was easy to see that he had been drinking again, that apparently he had been asleep. There was a stubble of beard on his face, which showed haggard and gray. But there was a new look in his eyes now, as, in silence, he surveyed the six men before him—the cowering sheriff,

Chisholm behind him, with Rafe, white-faced but steady, at the side. And the three gunmen from Sunset in a half-circle behind them.

'You—you boys better—go outside an'—and wait a while,' Forbes said, and his tongue rasped roughly across suddenly dry lips. 'While we—while we talk.'

It was Shorty, standing a massive six feet six, who answered him.

'This is bein' settled, here and now,' he snarled. 'We got our orders. If you wanted to be a fool, that's yore lookout!'

Silence came again, tense and harsh. Somewhere a fly buzzed, the sound unnaturally loud. They were set to kill, and, even with his own gun on Forbes, it was a hair-trigger tension. A very little could swing it now. Chisholm knew it, and in the silence, his voice even and courteous as ever, the judge spoke.

'You wished to see me, Mr Chisholm?'

'Yes, Your Honor,' Chisholm agreed, his own voice as matter-of-fact, 'about an annulment of the marriage, which was never a legal one in fact, of Molly Benton to Symes Gallister.'

There were ravages on the judge's face which had not been there before. Signs of struggle, of suffering, as though fine gold had come out of the fire refined and sure. He nodded carefully.

'I have been considering that,' he agreed, 'and it is time, in a very few minutes, to open court. Sheriff, if you will lead the way, please!'

There was silence again, a tautness in which no one stirred. And then one of the guards laughed.

'This is right funny—but it's gone far enough,' he gritted. 'Let's finish it, boys.'

That, Chisholm knew, was the signal—a cold-blooded decision which had already written the sheriff off as of no consequence. He had underestimated the quality of these killers, he knew, as Forbes had done himself. And now, though the numbers were about evenly divided, here in this room, with the sheriff too frightened to count either way, still the odds were all with those in the half-circle behind him. For if he made good his bluff and killed Forbes, that would mean that Rafe and himself would be riddled the next instant—before he could swing his gun, before Rafe could drag his own iron.

Yet the time had come, and the trio were calling the turn. There was no hope in him of winning, not at such odds. But there was always the chance to go down fighting, and he was doing that now. Twisting with that one hand upon the sheriff's arm, spinning the helpless Forbes around with such suddenness that he almost tripped and fell, placing him as a shield between himself and the bullets of the others—shifting his own aim and triggering all as a part of the same concerted movement.

His first shot took one of the other gunmen,

208

who seemed to be the fastest of the three. It ripped along his arm as he was lifting his weapon, plowing a furrow from wrist to shoulder, a gash which reddened as though a knife blade had ripped there, and sent the man staggering back to the wall, the fight all gone out of him.

But Rafe, though he had drawn pay for a while with Sunset, was not in a class with these gunmen, however stout his heart. He could not move fast enough to be helpful, and that left odds of two to one against Chisholm, and now both of them had their own guns out and spitting. And those, even now, were impossible odds.

Chisholm concentrated his attention on the huge Shorty. Once he had underestimated him, as only a cowhand, slow and clumsy. Shorty now was demonstrating how wrong he had been, though seeing him here as a guard had been warning enough. Big he was, but with a speed almost equal to Chisholm's own, and the deadly purpose of the born killer. It looked out of his eyes now, a hot and wicked light of fervid anticipation.

Chisholm knew that his own bullets were smacking into the big man, at that point-blank range—and that he was standing there and triggering back as though they had been bee stings and nothing more. And the other gunman, equally deadly, he could give no attention to at all.

In Chisholm's grasp, the shivering form of the sheriff went lax, was a drooping weight which he could no longer steady in front of him. The room was filled with the shattering din of guns, the harsh retching odor of burning powder. His own gun was empty, and the malignant giant still stood there and triggered back at him.

And then silence. In it, unbelievingly, Chisholm saw that Rafe was on the floor, but fumbling desperately for a dropped gun. Red dripped from his hand, but he paid no attention to it. And three men were sprawled there now, as the giant slumped across the sheriff. But before he could understand it, the door opened suddenly again and Symes Gallister stood there.

He had a drawn gun in his hand, and his glance swept the room with quick impersonal regard. Then he was lifting his own weapon, and, though he still held his gun, Chisholm knew that it was empty. The big man had been hard to down.

He waited for the shock of the bullet, hearing the thunder of guns in his ears, but it did not come. Strangely, it was Gallister who was down, a look of bewilderment large upon his face. Bewilderment, and frustration.

Chisholm turned then, aware for the first time that his own left arm hung limp, that a quick searching pain was growing in it, and he saw Judge Wood, the smoking gun in his hand

and a look almost of content on his face.

'Two,' he nodded. 'I'm still not too bad with a gun.'

He was silent a moment, then he spoke again, as though still half asleep and considerably surprised.

'The courthouse isn't far,' he said. 'We can make it in time. Come on.'

Rafe was getting to his feet then, and they walked across the street, a strange, oppressive silence following them, after the thunder of guns. Furtive faces peered from here and there on the street, but no one came close to look. There was a slow dignity to the way Judge Wood walked now that was doubly impressive, and Chisholm felt as if he was a part of the dream that seemed still to hold the jurist. They entered the dim cool recesses of the courthouse, the tiled floor echoing clammily to their footsteps. There was fresh blood flecking it as they went, Chisholm saw, and looked at his own bleeding arm, at the reddened hand of Rafe.

The bailiff, a look of fright upon his face, stood hesitant, until a word from Wood sent him scurrying to fling open the door. Very stately in his progress now, the judge crossed to his bench and took his seat, while the bailiff intoned the words that the court was now in session.

Then, a little wearily, Judge Wood stood up. And in that instant, Chisholm was aware that

Molly and Sandra Wood were in the room at the far entrance—frozen there as the judge rapped with his gavel. And behind them, John Thomas, with his glossy whiskers, and Superintendent Lang.

'Mr Chisholm,' Judge Wood said, 'there are certain matters to come before this court. Mr Bailiff, make note of them, in the absence of the clerk. I was intending to grant an annulment—but death has taken that out of my jurisdiction. For the other, since Sheriff Forbes no longer presses his charges, you, Mr Chisholm, are declared not guilty in the defensive killing of Jud Rance.'

For a moment longer he stood, while the hush continued. His gavel fell, rolled and bounded on the floor.

'Court—is adjourned,' he said huskily, and collapsed suddenly in his chair.

Sandra was the first to reach him, but the rest of them were close behind. Now, for the first time, Chisholm saw the gunshot wounds which at first had apparently bled only internally. Sandra's arms were about her father, and a look of content was on his face.

'Oh, Dad,' she cried. 'I—I'm sorry. I never understood—'

'It's—all right, Sandra.' He nodded. 'It took—what you did, to wake me up. Though I want you to know—that I did it—for you. I came here, to Red Rock—intending to be— square. But Gallister—had my record. I'd—

taken part in a bank hold-up—as a youngster. I—didn't know any better, then. And he threatened me—with the penitentiary.'

He looked at her, and his fine, leonine head was sagging a little, but there was pride in his eyes still.

'Don't worry about me,' he said, and for a moment his voice was stronger. 'Bill Gordy—is a mighty fine fellow. And I like it a lot better, this way, to go out—like a man!'

He smiled again, and leaned his head forward on the bench. Court had adjourned.

*   *   *

'Reckon I'll have to marry you, so I can kinda look after you,' Nellie conceded. 'You sure need somebody to do it for you, Rafe, I will say that much!' She nodded, and smiled a little, to where two dim figures moved under the moonlight.

'Anyway,' she added, 'marryin' seems to be a mighty popular notion, around here, all of a sudden. Sandra aimin' to change her name to Gordy, and Miss Molly, figgerin' on really sayin' yes to what the preacher asks, this time! Though with a man like Chisholm, I can't say I blame her a mite—Oh, go 'long with you, Rafe! Sure I do. Ain't I sayin' the same thing, too?'